Trauma Room Two

Trauma Room Two

Philip Allen Green

ISBN: 1511900024
ISBN 13: 9781511900027

For my family

These stories are fiction. I made them up. They are based on real experiences I have had working as a physician, but the characters, the specifics, even a few of the medical practices in the story are fiction, intentionally chosen for their narrative power. Any resemblance to people, living or dead, real or otherwise, is coincidental and unintentional.

Questions or Comments:

philipallengreen@hotmail.com

Table of Contents

Mistakes

Sometimes when I am bored, when it is all sore throats and dental pains, when I feel more like I am a social worker and a hand-holder than an emergency medicine physician, I play a game.

I do not look at the chart before I go into a room. I walk in cold. I enter with no idea who is going to be in there or why. In that very first second, before anyone speaks, I try to guess what the story is, who the people in the room are, and why they are in my emergency room.

Here—maybe it would make more sense if I showed you.

I draw back the curtain and step into Trauma Room Two. My eyes scan quickly about, gathering as much information as they can.

There are three people in the room.

For a brief second, I intentionally do not look at the patient lying on the hospital bed, not yet. Two people accompany the patient, a man and a woman. The man sits on a hard plastic chair pushed back against the room's wall, staring quietly ahead. I start with him. I know if I can just look closely enough, the story is there.

I study him. He is in his late forties. He wears a jet-black business suit. The fine fabric lies starkly against a bright, white, collared dress shirt. The dress shirt is pressed and starched and clean. He shifts slightly in the chair, and the red silk tie around his neck catches the light just so, drawing my eye to it. Small square gold icons fill the tie in an exact and set pattern. The knot at the top is tied with perfect precision and symmetry. This means something. I look more closely.

On his left wrist, he wears a Rolex. The bands are polished silver and cradle an oyster-white face on which three hands mark the time, the smallest of which ticks along, second by second by second. The outside of the watch face is meticulously trimmed in gold and clearly asserts to all who see it that this man's time is expensive.

As I observe, he moves his wrist a fraction of an inch, and the whole thing explodes into shimmers, sparkling magnificently from just the weak fluorescent lights overhead. It dawns on me that his watch alone costs more than the car I drove to work this morning. I cannot help but think, *"This man is nothing like me."*

I have learned I have to be careful with people like him. A single misstep in our interaction can easily result in a long string of complaint letters. But it is OK. I have done this enough that it does not frighten me or anger me or even annoy me. It is just a dance I have to be conscious of in this room. I make a mental note to be careful, and then continue my study.

Atop his head sits black hair with just a dusting of silver—executive hair, I believe it is called. It is thick and full and glowing with virility. Every strand is carefully combed into place. His hair shines nearly as brightly as his watch.

He lifts his head just slightly to look at me, and I notice a tiny cluster of hair is out of place. Just above and behind his left ear, the small bunch breaks from the linear strands around it, twisting up in disarray. It is not much, but it is there. On a man like him, it is nothing and everything at the same time.

Something is wrong.

His face is clean-shaven, the skin healthy and bright. Two black, sharp, crisp Italian eyebrows sit above pale blue, intelligent eyes that read me in a glance, as quickly as I read him. A strong jaw cuts the angle of his face into the space of the room around it. He does not need to smile for me to know his teeth will be perfect and symmetrical and white.

Under each eye hangs a faint dark circle. He has not been sleeping well. I am guessing, of course, but it looks to be more than just work fatigue. Perhaps a struggle outside of work has started to spill over into what must be an all-consuming drive for achievement. Or perhaps it is nothing other than the tracks left on him from another successful merger. I cannot tell—not yet.

It is strange to see someone like him here, even if he is just accompanying the patient. I am an ER doctor in a small emergency room, in a small hospital, in a small town, in the middle of nowhere. I can't help but wonder how a man like him ends up in an ER out here so far from the city. He does not have the look of someone who has come to hunt or fish, and he is definitely no wheat farmer. But something has pulled him here from far away, something that could not wait. I look closer.

The lines, curves, and circles of his face come together into an expression that is hard, at first, for me to read. I can sense he is a master at controlling what his face reveals. But my job is to read faces and bodies as well as he reads the stock market. In the curve of his mouth, I read frustration. In the angle of his brow, I read anger. In the tilt of his head, I read even a trace of fear.

But there is something else—something he does not want anyone to see. He hides it so well, after so much practice and time, I almost miss it. In fact, I am sure I would have missed it when I first started out, 41,422 patients ago. But that was then.

There, like a single, delicate, fleeting strand woven through a cloth of steel, is a tenderness and a sadness. What it is doing inside a man like him—I cannot comprehend. I can see why he wants to— no, why he *has* to—hide it in his world. He works to obscure it in the glint of his eyes and the shine of what must be a string of brutal successes. But still it is there.

Now that I see it, I see it clearly. It has blindsided him like a flash flood in the spring, sweeping him off his feet and tossing him down a canyon from which he cannot escape. He is drowning in this maelstrom of sadness, and no amount of money, power, or rage against the universe can make it abate.

An empty chair sits next to him.

One chair over is a woman.

She is slightly younger than the man.

I cannot see her face; her body is turned partially away from me.

She is resting her elbows on her knees, looking at the screen of her phone. She cradles it lovingly like a newborn. Marvelous red nails stand out against a white-and-gold iPhone. Her fingers are long and elegant like those of a famous pianist or a brain surgeon. She taps and slides the icons on the screen with elegance, as if they are servants being sent to do her bidding.

Her forearms are bare and hairless, but it is her biceps that stand out. They are small, solid, and precise, like an exclamation point stamped onto each upper arm. Biceps like that shout yoga, Pilates, personal trainers, green smoothies, and a lock on the bathroom door after big holiday meals.

Long brown hair is pulled back into a ponytail that falls gracefully to the middle of her back. A small silver clasp studded with diamonds traps the hair behind her head, holding it in place. It out-shimmers even the man's Rolex.

She wears a light gold, silk shirt. There is a cutout in the top back of it. I can just barely see her upper spine under the skin. Each vertebra makes a small bump in the arch of her lower neck, and each one is the exact same distance from the one above and below it. There are no outliers, no overly large or overly small bones. Each rise in her skin is exactly the same size and distance from the other. Before this moment, I did not realize bones in a back could be so flawless.

The skin over the bones is a rich, deep tan. It glows from her vegan diet and vitamin regimen. As she taps her finger on the phone, little ripples appear in the muscles of her back. I cannot help but stare in awe of such royalty stopping in our humble town.

She, too, is obviously nothing like me.

On the floor by her feet sits a purse. Its handle is a bent half circle of bamboo attached with gold and silver clasps to the bag below. The bamboo is polished and smooth. The wood is a blend of browns. A creamy white winds through the handle, somehow offsetting the dark tones and grains of the wood.

The purse itself looks to my unsophisticated eye not unlike the color of a wet pack horse after it has crossed a deep stream. It is a different shade of brown from the bamboo. It is like no brown I have ever seen before. As I look more closely, I see it is a bright, full, radiant brown that I can only compare to the soil on the edge of town in the spring. Soil that is freshly turned and waiting for seeds to spring up from it with life. Silver clasps and bamboo buttons adorn the purse in a perfect harmony of style. But there is something else—something that strikes me as oddly awful, something that should never be.

The purse has fallen over. The perfect brown of its side rests against our faded linoleum floor. Its contents spill out under the chair, untouched.

My second is almost up.

Now, at last, I turn to the patient.

A man lies on the bed. The pointed toes of scuffed cowboy boots stick up like two sharp rocks in a field. Straw and dirt pepper them and have shaken off onto the sheets. A pair of old blue jeans covers the top of the boots. They, too, have brought pieces of the farm and fields into the ER.

The man is supposed to be in a hospital gown. All our patients are. But more often than not, men around here will refuse to take off their boots and jeans. Sometimes I walk into rooms, and cowboy hats still sit perched atop heads. It is just part of living in this corner of the world.

The thighs of his jeans are faded where he must wipe his hands when in the fields. He must be right-handed, as the right thigh is faded much more than the left. A thick, worn leather belt with a buckle the size of two fists holds up jeans on a waist that is much too skinny.

The belt buckle is a flat grayish silver with an image stamped onto the front. A bronco bucks wildly, and a cowboy on top holds on with one hand strapped snug to the horse and the other in the air for balance. His hat is spiraling off his head into the air above him. "Pendleton Round-Up Champion 1942" is etched across the top, and the words "Let 'Er Buck" are below. In an odd way, I realize he, too, is nothing like me.

The man lies shirtless on the bed. The hairs of his chest are gray. A tattoo of marines raising the flag at Iwo Jima is inked just above his heart. The whole tattoo moves up and down with his gasping.

I look to his face.

It is tired and worn and ready to stop fighting. I see that multiple rounds of chemotherapy have taken all his hair, leaving behind nothing but eyebrows. His skin sags, and there is no light remaining in his eyes. They stare blankly ahead. Drops of sweat gather and cluster on his brow as I watch. The end is near.

The man and the woman stand up to join me at the bedside. The woman stands on one side, her diamond-clad hand gently resting on the old man's shoulder. The man who came with her stands on the other, his strong fingers lovingly resting on the thick skin of the old man's sunburnt neck.

I look from face to face to face, and I am surprised to see tears falling on every single one. The tears roll past similar noses, shared chins, and pale blue eyes. The pieces fall into place before me.

A daughter and a son have come home to say good-bye to their father.

I watch as the brother and sister sit down on either side of the bed. The old man, still gasping for air, suddenly sees them. With a struggle, he lifts his arms. The brother and sister lean in against their father. He lowers his arms across their shoulders as if they are still children. They rest their heads against his, curling up against his bony frame while he pants and waits for the end.

Standing before them, it suddenly hits me.

I have made a terrible mistake.

They are all just like me.

Transitions

Back when the color of blood was still bright to me, back when the sound of sirens made my heart race, back when I carried my ER skills like two loose six-shooter guns swinging from my hips, I would walk about the ER and say foolish things.

"Bring it on," I would say. "Bring it on."

I was fresh from residency, done with my training, a young doctor with a new white coat, ready to test myself and my skills against whatever the world threw at me.

"Bring it on," I said.

So the world did.

The world did.

———

She is seventeen. She is wearing a blue and white soccer outfit. It is still sweaty from practice. Her jersey has a big white number seven on the front of it. Just above the number is a tiger mascot. Its fangs are bared, its ears are back, and its legs are crouched, ready to pounce on all those foolish enough to challenge it.

There is a small number seven on each sleeve. Dime-sized soccer ball patches have been ironed on to the area around each number seven—I am guessing one ball for each goal scored. I want to stop and count the goals she has made, but I do not have time. "*Good Lord,*" I think to myself, "*she has scored a lot of goals.*" There are so many balls representing so many goals it is almost comical. They nearly cover the number seven. Lucky number seven.

Her hair is straight and brown. It is pulled back into a ponytail to keep it out of her face during practice. A little scrunchie, I think it is called, holds it in place.

I stand to her right. She arrived just a few seconds ago. Her facial skin is smooth with a few pimples on it, each of which has just a trace too much concealer over it. She has braces. Her face is the type that loves horses or cats or puppies or maybe all three. I can tell it has that happy kindness toward life that grows in the young when their world consists of birthday parties with balloons, loving parents, and caring teachers.

She likes bracelets. Not the fancy silver kind, but the cheap, plastic, rubber band–like ones that teenagers wear. Her whole right wrist is covered in bracelets as if they were actual rubber bands and she were heading out on the longest paper route in the world. Two eyes from an old Hello Kitty watch peek out through the bracelets.

I step to the head of the bed. A letterman's jacket has fallen off the gurney and lies on the floor. I see it has four soccer pins across the top of the big *V* for "Varsity." This must be her senior year. There are also four pins for track and four pins for basketball. She must be very busy.

I kick the jacket aside so that I can stand squarely at the head of the bed to direct the show. It is a chaotic scene—people are everywhere in Trauma Room Two, shouting in strained voices, banging equipment into walls, tearing open packages of tubes and lines and fluids in a frantic hurry.

"Parents are thirty-five minutes out!" someone yells.

She may be wearing some girlie things like bracelets and a Hello Kitty watch, but I do not want you to get the wrong impression of who she is.

This girl is a war-horse.

She is athletic. Crazy athletic.

Her right arm and leg in front of me are long with muscles that quiver and quake, ready to explode into action, ready to sprint across any soccer field in full-on attack mode, and ready to kick the game-winning goal with such force that the opposing goalie ducks out of the way.

I start my exam.

I examine her head. I shine my light into her right pupil first. It shrinks away from the light as a pupil should. I take the light away, and it expands. The reflex is strong and healthy, just like she was nineteen minutes and eighteen seconds ago.

I look in her right ear. The tympanic membrane is pink like the fingernails of her right hand. Actually, I take that back. Her fingernails are pink, but they have little sparkles in the paint that catch the light. Her right tympanic membrane does not sparkle. It is just pink. The outside of her ear is unremarkable. The bottom of her earlobe—or lobule, if you want to use a medical term—is pierced. A small silver soccer ball earring lies perfectly flush against the skin.

Somewhere in the back of my head, I imagine her face filled with surprise and delight as she opens a box containing little soccer ball earrings for her birthday. I wonder if it is a matching set or if on the other ear I will find a volleyball or perhaps a softball. It would not surprise me. She has varsity and college scholarships written all over her.

I listen on the right side of her chest. The lung is clear. Each breath sounds strong, radiant, and healthy. She could probably run a mile in under seven minutes with just her right lung alone. I lift my stethoscope out of the way as the trauma shears come chomping through her lucky-number-seven jersey. I watch as several of the soccer balls are cut into half-moons by the big silver blades.

I move on to her abdomen. The right side of it is nondistended and soft, as it should be. I can actually feel her liver, not because she is a drinker but because her body fat must be eight percent. If she were flexing her stomach muscles, I have no doubt the rounded lip of the lower edge of her liver would disappear under the rock-hard muscles that ripple just below the surface.

In my head, I see a soccer team in the August heat doing sit up after sit up out in the sun. Each time she sits up, I hear her yell to her teammates, *"This is our year for State! This is our year for State!"* They answer back with just as much fury, *"This is our year for State!"* A coach stands back, hands on his hips and admiration on his face, shaking his head in amazement. He has never had a player with such a drive, a determination, and an infectious ferocity to win.

The right side of her pelvis is stable. Her right hip bone sticks up as it should. I press down on it, checking for laxity or signs of a fracture. It does not give way or flex. Her pelvis is solid, at least on the right. The bones spring back as I let go, just as she probably does when an opposing player slide-tackles her to the turf.

She is wearing a pair of spandex running shorts under her soccer shorts. They are blue. They are tight on her right upper leg. The muscles, even now, retain their form, their long, linear lines the result of wind sprints, long distance runs, and day after day in the weight room dreaming of State. I hear her voice in my head. *"I will lead this team to State. I will lead this team to State,"* she says to herself during leg curl after leg curl on the same weight machine the football players use. She does it until she can barely move her legs and the muscles glisten with dreams.

I squeeze my gloved hands down her right leg, looking for trauma or a sickening crunch. I find neither. My hand fits only halfway around the muscles of her right quad. I think of endless squats in her room every morning before school. I can see her as she pushes herself to the limit, staring at the picture on the wall of her team accepting the second place trophy at the State Championship game last year.

But not this year.

"I will lead this team to State," she says. She has risen every day for the entire year at four thirty in the morning. She has run five

miles in the dark, through the rain, the snow, and the wind. She has pushed herself, her body, and her team to their utmost limits. She is the captain this year. She is the senior. She is the leader. *"I will lead this team to State,"* she says, hands on her knees, gasping for air under the streetlights in the December rain as the early morning paper boy rides by on his bike, shaking his head at the crazy girl in soccer shorts who just sprinted past him.

Her right knee is solid. No joint laxity. No ACL, MCL, or PCL tear in this knee will hold her back. Her right tibia is long and sharp on the front of her leg. With such long legs and such cut muscles, she must be hell on the field to try to defend. She can outrun 95 percent of the boys on the track team.

And still she is not satisfied.

"I will lead this team to State," she says each night in front of the mirror, staring at her reflection. She says it again and again as she falls asleep. It is the first thought through her mind the next day when she wakes.

I examine her right foot. She wears a blue and white Adidas soccer shoe that matches her team uniform. The cleats on the bottom are just starting to wear. I am guessing she gets new shoes fairly often to train in. The whole team depends on her. She is the star, the alpha, and the reason that in eight days her team will play in the State Championship game for the second year in a row.

One glance at her, and it is easy to tell that she is the reason the college scouts were everywhere at the playoffs this year. They all wanted a glimpse of the girl who could lead a team and push herself like a champion. No—no worn shoes would do for these feet. Too much rides on them for too many people.

"I will lead this team to State." I hear it in my head one last time.

I step back to the head of the bed.

I now begin examining her left side.

Her hair is stuck to her face on the left. A plastic endotracheal tube extrudes from her mouth, breathing for her. I ignore it. I shine my light into her left pupil. It is a giant black hole, sucking all championships away, taking all her team with it, taking all those whose lives she has touched into an empty, bottomless blackness.

Her pupil is blown. It does not respond to the light that I shine into it because somewhere in her brain something is bleeding and expanding, smashing and squishing her potential up against the limited space of her skull. All of who she is and who she could be is disappearing second by second into that abyss.

I pull back the dried-up hair over the left ear. It is stiff and in clumps where it has dried. I have to pinch it and pull it off the skin. It sticks out like dry pasta, crackling as I force it to bend out of the way.

I look in her left ear. The tympanic membrane is purple. There is blood behind it, pushing against it. She has a basilar skull fracture somewhere in the distance, past the eardrum. It looms like the end of her future, just out of sight.

I palpate the back of her cervical spine. Her neck is thin. I imagine it whipping around in a fury on teammates who do not pull their weight or give their best. *"This is our year for State!"* she used to scream. At first some girls would cry when she yelled at them, but over time they all began to believe. *"This is our year for State!"* they would yell back, pushing themselves as hard as they could, trying to keep up with their fearless captain.

Each little bump of her cervical vertebrae follows the next. Bump by bump, I feel down her vertebrae like a blind man reading giant Braille. Then one stands out, out of place, an outlier.

Cervical vertebrae protect the spinal cord. When the bones move, the spinal cord underneath does too. Spinal cords are not meant to shift about. Sometimes, when exposed to too much force, they do not spring back into place. Instead, the bones cut, sever, or slice the spinal cord just underneath them. My fingers tell me the bone is so far out of place that even if the world's best neck surgeon were here in our little ER, he or she could do nothing.

I move to the left side of her chest. When I place my stethoscope on the skin, it crunches like Rice Krispies. Even the tiny weight of my stethoscope is too much, and I feel her chest give way. The ribs must be shattered, the lung burst. I listen. Her breathing sounds are distant, crackly, and dark—if there is such a sound.

It dawns on me that she really is breathing on her right lung alone. Right now her body is running the equivalent of a four-minute mile on that one lung. I can hear her left lung bubbling. It is full of fluid—the fluid that comes when a lung is smashed like an old state record by a champion athlete.

I push on the left side of her abdomen, my fingers seeing inside. It is already more distended than it was just thirty seconds ago. The ribs along the bottom left of the rib cage give way just enough to make me feel sick. Her left rib cage is the goalkeeper to her spleen, and this time it has failed. I do not need an ultrasound or a CT scan to know that her spleen has exploded. Exploded, just as the crowd did, when she scored the goal in the last minute of the game that carried her team into the State Championship this year.

"We will not be denied!" she had screamed to her team.

"This is our year for State!" they had screamed back.

Her pelvis is still stable.

That's good. I guess.

She has a large piece of sharp metal embedded in her left groin. It pulsates with the femoral artery it has partially severed underneath. *"How did she even survive the ambulance ride here?"* I wonder. The biggest medic in town leans over her, forcing all his weight through a balled-up fist against her groin, trying to occlude the vessel. He drips with sweat from the effort. Just below his hands, the left quadriceps muscle has a white bone sticking up through it.

"Where is the surgeon?" I yell.

"He is elbows deep in a septic belly in the operating room!" someone yells back.

"Where is the other surgeon?" I ask.

"He's out of town," someone else says.

"How far out is the helicopter!" I yell.

"No go. Medics already called. It's too windy for them to fly today," another voice quietly answers.

I suddenly feel very alone in the world.

"*Goddamn small towns*," I think.

The giant medic pushes down as hard as he can. But he has to push against an elite cardiovascular system pumping furiously from adrenaline. Blood does not ooze out like an old lady with a trickling nosebleed. If the medic moves his hands at all, it will spray out like a fire hose at full bore.

"*How is she still alive?*" I wonder. She must have lost an incredible amount of blood on the scene.

Then, as if answering my question, she codes.

"Where are her parents?" I yell again, my voice trembling this time.

"Thirty minutes out!" someone else yells back.

"Well, tell them to hurry the hell up," I say.

I try to run the code as she ran through state records: I give it my all, my very best. I dig deep, pushing my team and myself beyond our comfort levels. I do everything I know to do. I ask everyone in the room for ideas when I run out. I do not want to stop. I do not want to take away a future that burns so very, very brightly. I do not want to be the one who pulls the plug.

But I am.

By the time I finally say, "Stop," there is more blood outside of her than inside of her. It is a terrible thing.

We have used up all the blood in our little hospital in fifteen short minutes. It went in, and it came out.

She has died.

"The parents are here—the parents are here," a breathless woman from registration says.

"*They are three goddamned minutes too late*," I think to myself.

Now it is time for me to talk with her parents.

I slowly take off my trauma gown, the blue fluid proof material stained a bright red. I take off my mask. I take off my gloves. Both are soaked in her blood from the last-ditch, Hail Mary attempts to keep her alive.

The problem with Hail Mary passes is that they rarely work in the real world.

I ask a nurse who stands back, her face still stunned, "Do I look OK?"

She stares at me for a second. She knows what I mean. She grabs a towel and wipes off the blood that has splashed across my face. I ask her to check one more time, just to be sure. She is sure. There is no blood, no tiny drops, not a molecule her dad or mom will have to see on me.

Sometimes being a doctor is the loneliest feeling in the world. The staff and nurses give me space. They step back, pretending to be busy as they shuffle papers, untangle lines, and start cleaning up the floor.

I appreciate that. I appreciate the moment to get myself ready.

I walk down the hall that leads to the family room. It is empty. There are no patient rooms or people. I can hear my steps echo on the linoleum floor. The walls have no windows. I cannot look out and dream of the mountains to the south. It is just me, walking down a hall by myself.

I try not to think about my own daughter, my own sons. I try not to think about what it is I am about to do. I try not to think about how awful it would be to receive college acceptance letters when the applicant no longer resides at the residence.

I open the door. The parents sit on the couch side by side, arm in arm, as soccer players do on the bench, in the last game of the year, in the last second, down by one, still hoping against hope for a win, a miracle.

But not today.

Over time I will forget the blood in her hair, the crushed chest, the broken femur, and the severed artery. They will blur with the other injuries I carry in my head. But I never forget faces. Faces that begged me to tell them a miracle, to tell them we saved their daughter, to tell them there is still hope.

I sit down across from them. My right hand begins to tremble. I fold my left hand over it to hide it. I take a deep breath. I focus. I speak.

"Your daughter was hit by a drunk driver walking home from practice. We did everything we could—everything there is to do and then some. But she has died. She has died."

My words transition them. Transition them from a family back to a couple. I try not to think about that. But I cannot always control what I think.

I used to search for something more to say. Something wise, something profound, and something comforting. Anything. Anything at all. But I have done it enough times now to know there is nothing else to say.

I watch their entire universe collapse in on itself. It explodes apart in front of me. Their lives disintegrate and scatter, like dust in the wind, into a thousand pieces, a thousand directions. My three words obliterate everything about who they are, who they were, and who they will be.

I sit, squeezing my right hand as hard as I can so that it will stop trembling. I press my fingernails into my palm until it hurts, and then I press some more. I force my mind to the side, to a far off place in my head.

"Not now," I tell myself, "not now." I will think about this later. Right now I have to keep it together. I am fifty-eight minutes into the start of a twelve-hour shift, day one of a seven-day stretch of work. There are fourteen more patients checking in. We are behind now from dealing with this trauma. I am the only doctor in this ER. I cannot think about this right now. I must not think about this right now.

Pastoral services arrive. They take over sitting with the parents. I will swing by Trauma Room Two in a few minutes when the parents go in to say good-bye. I want to be there for that. It is my duty to be there, to stand quietly in the corner while they weep. To help them say good-bye. To answer any questions they have. To be one more person who will never forget their daughter.

I walk back down the hall. Girls in soccer uniforms are running past me toward the family room, sobbing. They already know. Another girl's parents go running past me toward the family room. A set of grandparents go running past me toward the family room. Coaches and trainers go running past me toward the family room. They are all meteors falling from the sky around me, one by one by one.

But I have work to do. I cannot think about this right now. "*Not now—not now*," I tell myself.

I step into the next patient's room. I sit down. Their daughter has ear pain. She is four years old. She runs about the room, her hair pulled back in a ponytail—held in place with a scrunchie.

Her parents make a joke about the long wait to be seen this morning. They are trying to be funny, pleasant, and friendly. I appreciate that, more than they will ever know.

I try to smile. I try to play along. "*Not now, I tell myself,*" not now.

I survive the shift. I walk in the door to my house twelve hours later.

My kids run over and hug me. My wife asks, "How was your day?" Before I can answer, my youngest bangs his head on the counter and cries. My wife kneels down and gives him a kiss.

"Fine," I lie. "Work was fine."

"Can you take the boys to soccer practice?" she asks. "Oh, and guess who got sent to the principal's office today." She gives me that look and then looks at our oldest boy. "Can you talk to him?"

"OK," I say, fighting the images threatening to erupt out of my head.

"Oh, one more thing. We got that bill for your dentist visit. They screwed up our insurance again. Can you call them when you get a chance, maybe at soccer practice? I told them you would call. I think the woman's name is Sherry. Ask for Sherry when you call."

"OK."

I walk down the hall of our house. "*Not now*," I tell myself, "*not now*." Keep it locked away. Keep it far from here.

That night, I can't sleep. I get up and pace about our house. It is dark. It feels empty even with my family here. I feel anxious and sweaty.

"*Not now*," I tell myself, "*not now*."

I take an Ativan and fall sleep.

The next day, I go to work.

Six days later I finish my stretch. Work spits me out the back end. I am chewed up. My head aches all the time. My joints don't feel like they come together right. I try to go for a run, but my body parts have somehow forgotten how to move together. I break out in a rash on my chin. I don't sleep more than an hour at a time. But I have survived my stretch of work. I have kept it together, I have done my duty, and I have finished.

It is my day off, but for the rest of my family, it is a workday and a school day. They are gone by the time I wake up.

I make a peanut butter and jelly sandwich and pack it in my backpack. I get on my motorcycle and ride for two hours up dirt roads out into the mountains.

I find a quiet spot that looks out over some canyons, and I make a small campfire. I make some tea—green mint tea, and throw some pine needles into the hot water.

When it is done, I walk over to the edge of the canyon, my little tin cup steaming with the smell of mint and pine. I sit down with my back against an ancient tree.

And I open the box in my head.

One by one I take out and inspect the girl, her parents, the ER, myself, my family, this town, and this life.

Like precious rocks gathered from the bottom of a river, I hold them up in my head, turning them round and round in the bright sunlight, inspecting them, trying to understand them.

They are pieces of a puzzle that I cannot fit together. I try different combinations, different possible matches, but none work. No matter how I arrange them, the edges do not align; some uncomfortable space still sits between each and every one of them.

After a while, I stop. I sip my tea and watch a hawk ride a thermal round and round. Maybe the pieces are better left apart. Maybe my problems come from trying to put them together. I think to myself, maybe that's it, but it makes me anxious to have a box of loose puzzle pieces shaking about in my head.

But so be it.

The next day, I am preparing to start another stretch of work. I finish my coffee and set the cup in the sink when I see the front page of the paper on the kitchen counter.

I gasp out loud, and my right hand starts to tremble.

In a big photo filling half the page is a girls' soccer team. They stand on a stage that has been set up in the middle of a soccer field. They wear blue and white uniforms. There are tiger icons on the fronts of their jerseys.

I lean in, examining the photo. Next to each tiger, a small patch with the number seven has been sewn into the left chest of each girl's jersey. A giant gold trophy sits on the stage in front of them. Each girl is down on one knee with her head bowed, her right arm raised up, and her index finger pointing to the sky.

The team's goalie stands in the middle. Her head is bowed just like the others. But both her arms are raised up. Each of her hands grasps the bottom of a framed number seven jersey, holding it up above her head, holding it above them all.

I touch the picture with my fingers to make sure it is real.

It is.

"STATE CHAMPIONS AT LAST!" the headline screams above the photo.

I stand for a moment staring, alone in the kitchen, my heart racing. The spaces between the puzzle pieces in my head suddenly aren't quite as crippling as they were just a moment before.

"You did it," I whisper to the number seven jersey in the frame. "You led your team to State, just like you always said you would. You did it, and they won. Now go."

"Go, and rest in peace."

Night Shift

It is exactly six o'clock in the morning.

There is one hour left until the end of night shift.

It is a rainy Tuesday in February.

I sip my coffee and watch the raindrops splash down in the puddles of the ambulance bay. It is pitch black out. The security lights cut a white beam out into the rain and fog, disappearing into the dark.

I take another sip of my coffee. It has a deep, dark, rich taste that is magical at this hour. I sip it again, slowly, savoring the heat of the glass cup burning against the palms of my hands.

One hour to go.

The ER is empty. Housekeeping finished up a little while ago. The floors of Trauma Room Two and the rest of the ER have been scrubbed clean of blood, vomit, and excrement. The black mud every patient and family member tracked in last night has been wiped away. The floors are once again shiny and white, catching the parallel lines that are the reflection of the fluorescent lights buzzing quietly overhead.

In the rooms, each bed is prepared for the day with a single thin, white, rough cotton sheet. Each one is pulled tight and flat across a hard, black, plastic mattress. A pillow has been placed for a head at the top of each gurney.

The TVs in the rooms are off. No *Judge Judy*, no *Jerry Springer*, no CNN or Fox News blares out into the ER. No cell phones ring, no alarm bells sound, and no call lights buzz.

Everything is quiet.

Calm.

Still.

I rattled the gurneys at five o'clock this morning. Because of the rain, I let the drunks sleep in an extra hour. I shook their beds as they yawned and rubbed their bloodshot eyes and bearded faces. They did not argue or ask for a sandwich or even say thanks. It was all they could do just to rise and face the day. They knew it was an unspoken favor for them to get to sleep in, a temporary truce between us, a special exception when it is raining this hard.

They rose and wandered off, one by one, into the rain and dark. They reminded me of the elk I sometimes come across in the mountains just outside of town. As they left they moved slowly, deliberately, and carefully. I realized they search and pick their way through life, each looking for the next meal or drink—the next score.

I watch as the last one of them stops just outside the big glass ambulance door. He digs through the garbage can, foraging for glass to recycle, hoping to trade it in for a few pennies or maybe a dollar. But this time there is none to be found. He shakes the rain from his head, reshoulders his pack, and follows the rest of his herd off into the darkness, going wherever it is they go when they leave here.

I lean back, up against the bank of medic radios behind me. After a night of squawking out call after call, they are quiet. I take another sip. A nurse sitting down at the far end of the station looks at something on a computer. A green palm tree and blue sky fill the monitor. She clicks on a banner, surely dreaming about somewhere far, far away.

A few feet away sits another nurse. He is in his fifties. His hair is gray. He has a white hospital blanket wrapped tightly around his shoulders. His feet are crossed, resting up on the chair next to him. He hangs his head to the side. He is sleeping. I watch as his feet and hands twitch. Perhaps he is dreaming of the newborn baby we saved last night.

Every part of this ER is ready for the new day. In twenty minutes the day shift nurses will start to wander in. Everything will start anew. We of the night shift will pass this place back to them. Soon enough the patients will come, stacking up ten deep in the waiting room. Ambulances will roar into the bay, families will cry, babies will scream, and most patients will be saved—but some will die.

The day shift staff will run, rush, and do their best to stay afloat. They will grow tired, weary, and frustrated, just as we were a few hours ago when the ER was full. When we see them again in twelve hours, they will look like we look now, with our grizzled faces and tired eyes.

When we return tonight, this place will be different from the way it is now; it will be packed with patients and noise. But for now, for this one brief moment in time, the ER is quiet.

I take another sip of my coffee. It is almost gone. The rain sprinkles on the puddles outside.

"*Yes*," I think.

If you know where to look, you can find peace everywhere, even here.

The Crew

The deer jumps. It pushes off from the rain-soaked dirt, leaping into the sky. It rises, and it falls, descending directly into the bright white headlights of the oncoming Toyota Camry.

To the driver, it appears to drop from above, as if released from a giant's hand hovering just out of sight above the backcountry road. Its hooves clack on the pavement as it lands, and long legs bend down to absorb its weight. Linear shadows scatter across its flank from the speeding headlights of the oncoming car. The muscles of its back begin to contract in the light, flexing, preparing to launch itself back into the sky for the other side of the road.

The driver panics. At seventy-six miles per hour, there is no time to do anything, let alone brace for impact. The deer strikes the grill. The headlights disappear for a brief instant, replaced with a shower of red-and-white death as the deer disintegrates into the night.

The driver reacts, but it is too late. He turns the steering wheel away from the deer. The deer that no longer exists in this world. The car begins to slide. The driver's panic takes over, and he turns the steering wheel sharply back in the other direction. He turns toward the road, away from the white aspens now flashing past the headlights like piano keys falling from the sky.

The sliding wheels bite the pavement, and the pavement bites back. The car flips, end over end over end. When it stops, it is no longer a car but a twisted tomb of steel—dripping oil, bleeding gas, and steaming hot radiator fluid into the cold night air. Three of the four teenagers, still dressed in their prom clothes, are no more.

For a moment, nothing moves inside the car. All is silent. A quiet cry breaks the stillness. The heap of metal rattles and shakes slightly. A lone boy in a torn tuxedo crawls out of the crumpled rear window. He drops to the ground before collapsing onto his back in the dirt. He lies there, staring at the twinkling stars just visible through the small clearing in the clouds above. He pants, his heart pounding, as he listens to the *tap-tap-tap* of one of the wheels still spinning on what is left of the inverted car.

It is 1:38 a.m. on a Saturday in a small town everywhere.

———

"Doc." Hands shake me. "Doc. Wake up. We got a trauma."

I sit up on the side of the bed and rub my face. It is unshaven and rough. My mouth is dry from too much coffee. I was having a dream about our old dog. He was swimming in a lake for sticks. He never did that when he was alive. I look over at the clock. It is 2:04 a.m. Ugh.

I walk out into the hall. The night nurse, Susan, is flipping on the lights. The ER is coming to life. A recorded voice blares out from the speakers overhead.

"Attention. Trauma team to ER." The voice pauses and then repeats, "Attention. Trauma team to ER."

I laugh in spite of myself. Our trauma team at night is four people. When I worked in the city, the trauma team consisted of around twenty different specialists, techs, nurses, administrators, and surgeons. Day or night they came. Many times there were so many people present wanting to help that I had to kick some of them out of the room in order to make space for the patient.

Out here the trauma team is different. It consists of a doctor (that would be me), the ER nurse, a respiratory tech, and a floor nurse sent down from upstairs.

I walk over to the medic radio, listening for any radio chatter. It is quiet for now.

"What do we got?" I ask Susan.

She shakes her head. She is the ER night shift nurse. "We got four teenagers. Three dead on scene. One still alive. They are bringing him in."

My chest tightens.

I have three teenagers.

It is the end of a Friday night in our little town. It is prom. All three of my boys went to the dance. I run some quick odds in my head. There are eighty-six kids in the high school here. That means there is a three-in-eighty-six chance one of those dead kids is mine. Or if you prefer proper mathematics, a one-in-twenty-eight chance.

Not so good.

I scramble to remember what my wife said each of the kids was doing tonight after the dance. I look at my watch. They should all be arriving home by now. But they are teenagers, and it is prom. What do teenagers do after a dance? I shudder. I was a teenager once.

I get that feeling in the pit of my stomach that has come every weekend since my kids started high school. The Friday-Night-Pit, I call it. This is the only ER in town. I am the only ER doctor awake in the county right now. Every time the medic radio blares out about a car accident or a trauma, I find myself afraid. One question keeps coming up in my head: *Could I do it?* That is, could I code my own kid?

I know that is an upsetting question, one no one should ever have to ask, let alone think about. Yet it is part of my life and part of living in rural America. It is a real, solid, and cold fear that I face all the time.

"Could I do it?" I ask myself. *"Will I have to do it tonight?"*

I start to sweat.

"Where's the wreck?" I ask.

The nurse is doodling on a piece of paper.

"Hey. Susan. Where's the crash?"

She looks up. "Sorry, back side of Jackson Mountain."

She says it, but she is not listening. It dawns on me that she has a teenage daughter who goes to school with my children.

She is asking herself the same questions.

I am not a religious man. I do not go to church on Sundays as I probably should. But I would bet that, when I am at work, I pray more than just about any churchgoer. I pray quietly now, *"Please, God. Do not let any of them be one of mine."*

Is that a bad thing to pray for? Is it bad to pray that someone else's child is dead in a smashed-up car in a field alone in the dark, instead of my own? What does God think of that prayer? I don't know, but I pray it anyway.

"Please, God, let it be someone else's child."

By the expression on Susan's face, I know she is praying for the same thing.

"How far out?" I ask.

"Ten minutes."

"You said a boy was the survivor?"

She nods slowly.

I know she is thinking of her daughter.

I hear a key rattle in the back hallway door. It opens, and Tom, the respiratory tech, comes jogging down the hall. His hair stands up all catawampus, and a big crease runs down the side of his face from where it pressed against something while he was sleeping. He's a big guy, round and jolly, with a desire to jump in and help no matter what the task. If I put a patient on a ventilator, he is the one who runs the machine that keeps the patient breathing.

"What's up, Doc?" He smiles. Sweat shines on his forehead from the run down the hall.

I tell him. The smile disappears. "Shit," is all he says. He runs his hand over his forehead, wiping the sweat back into his hair. The jolly demeanor is gone. His son is a senior with my oldest. They play baseball together. Last year his boy hit a home run and got the team to the play-offs. He's a good kid.

The medic phone rings. I pick it up. It is dispatch.

"Doc, it's Ann. They are on the back side of Jackson. The radio on the rig is not working again. I will call you if I find out something more."

I hang up. Now we wait.

Jackson Mountain is one of the mountains that sits just south of town. It straddles two counties, both of which are mostly forest. It is not really a mountain in the traditional sense, but that is what all the kids around here call it. Everyone in town knows what goes on up at Jackson. We all know because we were kids once, too.

Up the winding gravel roads is a series of creeks, draws, and fields tucked back into scattered forests. It is a huge area at the edge of an even bigger spread of national forest land. It is an ideal place for bonfires, kegs, make-out sessions, and everything else teenagers like to do when there are no parents around.

The problem is that there are only two sheriffs for close to one thousand square miles of forest. One works in our county, and the other in the adjoining one. As you can guess, they don't spend a lot of time scouring the woods for parties. They have enough to deal with out here in the towns.

Jackson Mountain is a beautiful place. I loved Jackson Mountain when I was in high school, but dear God, do I hate it now. In the fifteen years I have been back in town, I have cared for more than my share of alcohol-fueled deaths of drivers from the windy roads running down the hills.

The elevator dings in the back of the ER, and its doors open.

Amanda is here. She is one of the night floor nurses. She is a chain-smoking, fried-food-eating, bean pole of a woman. But she is one hell of a nurse. She has a teenage daughter as well. In fact, I just saw her daughter right before the shift. My youngest is taking her to prom.

Amanda walks over, smelling like smoke. I wonder if she was sneaking a cigarette in the staff bathroom upstairs again. She sees our faces.

"Uh-oh," is all she says.

We tell her. I watch as she takes a deep breath, clasps her hands together, and marches off into Trauma Room Two. It is time to get ready.

This is it. The trauma team. We are the catchers in the rye out here. This tiny little group of four. We are all there is for a hundred-mile radius. And there is no one for us but one another.

First we gown and glove. No one speaks. I tie the back of Tom's gown and turn around, and he ties the back of mine. Amanda ties the back of Susan's gown and turns around, and Susan ties the back of hers. I pick up the box of masks with the clear plastic face shields. I hand them out one by one before putting on my own.

Tom and Amanda wheel out the gurney and pull the trauma bed into the room. It is much stiffer than a regular bed. It is made so an x-ray can be slid under the patient to take pictures without anyone having to move the patient off the bed. It also is stiff so we can do chest compressions without the patient sinking down into the mattress. It is fluid-proof so that, if need be, we can cut open a chest and put tubes into it or even try to fix an impaled heart while we wait for the medevac helicopter. It is made to withstand the doing of terrible things, all in the hope of achieving something wonderful.

When people imagine what it is like in an ER, they like to think of high fives, fist pumps, and amazing saves. They think that is what makes doctors, nurses, and emergency personnel such a close-knit group. But it is not.

It is moments like this. It is standing around an empty gurney together while we think about our own sons and daughters.

We wait. No one speaks.

I pray again, *"Please, God, do not let one of the dead be mine. And please, I beg you, do not make me run the code on my own child. Do not ask this of me."*

What is strange is that I know I could do it. I know I could cut off all my emotions and run the code with an ice-cold precision if I had to. I have a well-worn switch inside me that I flip on, shutting off my feelings at will.

But it comes at a price.

Over the years I have learned the hard way that each time I throw the switch, it becomes more difficult to turn it back off. If a case is too traumatic, too upsetting, and I close off all emotions, it can be weeks before the feeling part that makes me who I am returns.

If I had to code one of my own family members, I would do it. I have never had to throw the switch all the way, but if one of my family members came in, I would have to in order to run the code. I keep the switch ready inside me, day or night. Part of me knows that if I ever have to throw the switch all the way, it will be the end of me.

Don't get me wrong; I could do it in a second. I know because I force myself to practice it in my head over and over and over, so that if the day comes, I can do it and save them. I will not be the one who fails them when they need me the most.

"What kind of car was it?" Amanda asks quietly.

She stands with her gloved fingers interlaced in front of her. I realize she is praying that it is not her child. It strikes me that, in an odd way, she is praying that it is my child and not hers. I do not hold it against her. We of the ER face the darkness together in a way few others will ever know.

"They didn't say," I answer.

I see Tom texting on his phone. He is texting something over and over. Whoever is on the other end is not texting back. His eyes glisten just a shade, and his face pulls tight before he takes a deep breath and puts his phone away.

I am tempted to text my boys or my wife. But if they do not answer, then what? I would rather just be ready for anything. That is my job. That is what I am paid to do.

So here we are. There are eighty-six kids in our town's only high school. Between the four of us, we have six teenage children in the school. That is even worse odds. That is a one-in-fourteen chance that one of our kids was in that car. The Friday-night fear in the pit of my stomach grows. Those are bad odds.

I feel sick. *"Please, God. Don't let it be one of mine. Let my kids be home safe. Do not make me throw the switch all the way tonight. I can still help people. Give me this chance."*

Amanda looks like she is going to throw up.

"We have to stop meeting like this," I joke quietly. Everyone snickers. "Someday, someone is going to find out about the four of us."

Amanda relaxes slightly. "We are The Crew," she says.

"The crew that do," we all say together.

It is an old private joke between the four of us. At one time it was hilarious. But now it is who we are, and it is a quiet comfort in the middle of the night.

We hear sirens in the distance.

We look at one another. Sometimes, of all the people in my life, I feel the closest to those I hardly know outside of work.

We make a couple of quick, last-minute adjustments to Trauma Room Two. We are ready. I trust my crew. I know they will sacrifice themselves, no matter what comes through the door in the next thirty seconds. They are battle tested. They are blood-borne. They are family.

The ambulance arrives in the bay. The sirens stop. The sliding doors open.

I throw the switch inside me halfway, just enough, just in case God is not listening to my prayers tonight. My hand dangles over the switch, ready to push it to that one place I never want it to go. I will not look at his face, I tell myself. If it is my own son, I will not look at his face. I will throw the switch all the way and do what needs to be done. I run through it in my head as I have practiced, and I know I am ready. My doubts leave me. I empty myself. Whatever part of me feels, ceases to be.

The patient gurney rattles as they push it through the entrance. I do not hear a ventilator beeping or the *thump-thump-thump* of chest compressions.

"Let's do this," I say quietly.

They wheel the stretcher into the room.

A tuxedoed boy I do not recognize is sitting up on the gurney. There is blood splattered across his face and tuxedo but I do not think it is his. He is crying. He looks uninjured.

The medic who coaches my boys in basketball speaks the only words we are all listening for.

"Out-of-town kids. Out-of-town kids."

And in that moment, I know that he prayed the same prayer as we did. Only he prayed it racing up Jackson Mountain on the way to the wreck, with the lights and sirens blaring above him. He prayed that it was not his child who was in the accident. But he also prayed that if it was, that he could do it—that he could throw the switch all the way and do what needed to be done, regardless of the cost to himself. He, too, is part of the crew that do.

We all breathe a sigh of relief.

God has heard our prayers.

———

One county over, a sheriff stands outside a small house in the dark. Rain pours from the night sky. It collects on the brim of his hat before rolling down in great beads off the edge of it and onto his face and rain slicker.

A basketball sits in the driveway beneath a hoop above the garage. A soaking wet flag displaying his son's high school mascot drips from a flagpole by the door. The sheriff's wife sleeps inside, oblivious to the storm.

The sheriff is shaking ever so slightly, but not from the cold. He is the only sheriff on duty in all of Whiskey County tonight. The county that sits next to ours.

He, too, responded to the wreck.

He shakes.

He had to throw the switch all the way tonight.

It is 3:14 a.m. on a Saturday, in a small town, everywhere.

Saviors

One time I did something stupid.

I tried to count how many dead babies I have held in my own two hands.

That night, they visited me in my sleep. Gray babies. Blue babies. Floppy babies, stiff babies. Big babies, small babies, ugly babies, cute babies. Babies in diapers, babies in tiny dresses with little pink bow ties on their heads, babies blackened by house fires, babies whitened by hypothermia, babies I cannot write about because it is just too terrible to put to paper some of the babies I have seen.

I tossed and turned. I did not sleep.

And then, the very next shift, another dead baby came in.

The tires screeched. I looked up from the desk just in time to see a car skid to a stop in the ambulance bay. It was an old car—a beater. A Chevy Nova. It was pea-soup green, dirty, and dented. It was packed full of people. After skidding to a halt, it rocked back and forth from the momentum, teetering on a broken and useless suspension system.

The right rear door opened. "Rock You Like a Hurricane" by the *Scorpions* blasted out full bore from the stereo. A woman got out and stood up. She appeared to be in her twenties. Her arms were spindly and long like a spider's two front legs. Tiny track marks covered the skin of both upper extremities. Long lines of little black scars lay dotted in rows where needles had bit her one too many times as she searched for fresh veins and new highs.

The skin on her forearms was scabbed and pockmarked. She was a picker, a tweaker, a hopper, a junkie, a carpet crawler, a jibby, a crankster, a skitzer, a toothless and ruthless, a battery bender, a spinster.

She was what we in the business call a methamphetamine addict.

Everything about her had the look. The look of a junkie. A sharp, small nose, pointed from the center of her face, like an accusatory finger raging at the world. On her nose a bright orange septum ring looped up, disappearing into one of her flaring nostrils. Four plastic earrings stacked up the back of her left ear, and five more climbed the right. Each earring was a different color from the one next to it—like little rainbows of joy on the sides of her head. She grimaced. Most of her teeth were gone.

Meth mouth, we call it.

Her hair looked like rags tied to a pole. Ragged, if you will. It was blonde once, but dirt had brushed it brown. I watched her spin back around toward the rear seat. Her clumpy hair flew about her, radiating outward like some sort of woven dress on a whirling dervish.

My heart began to race. I took a step toward the ambulance bay. The sensor above detected me and the big glass door slid open. Somehow, I already knew what she would grab from the backseat in such a hurry, from such a car, on such a day.

A pair of arms from a man I could not see in the backseat held out what looked like a small package wrapped in a blue blankie. The woman standing outside the car grabbed the package. She screamed something to the driver. As if answering, the car's engine screamed back, and the rear tires spun, spitting clouds of dark smoke into the bay. The Chevy Nova leaped forward, and the sudden acceleration slammed its rear door shut with a bang. It was gone.

The woman did not notice. She was already running toward me. As she ran, the blankie fell from the package in her arms and landed in a pile on the ground. I stared at what remained in her grasp. It was not a package after all. It was the only thing it could have been.

A baby.

A dead baby.

A gray, lifeless baby.

She cradled it in her arms like a loaf of stale bread. She held the back of the baby's head awkwardly in the palm of her hand, its spine lying along the skin of her pockmarked forearm. As she ran, little arms and legs flopped about like a rag doll's.

There was hope.

It was not stiff.

She thrust the baby into my arms. It was still warm. Add another sliver of hope. I ran into Trauma Room Two with the woman following right behind. "Call the code!" I yelled as I passed the desk, holding the lifeless baby. So the secretary did. "Code pink, Trauma Room Two. Code pink, Trauma Room Two," the voice rang out overhead.

I set the gray baby down on the white sheet. Its arms flopped straight out to the sides—like a tiny Jesus on the cross. Deep green eyes stared unblinkingly at the ceiling of Trauma Room Two as if the baby were stunned speechless by the brutality of life.

It was not breathing.

It was pulseless.

It was a boy.

He had a big, round belly that stuck up. He had delightfully fat fingers and legs. His skin was smooth, and aside from its gray pallor, appeared healthy. A small patch of shiny black hair sat atop his head like a tiny sleeping cap. It was clear someone had been taking good care of him.

Add another sliver of hope.

His little body lay there, neither moving nor breathing, as the seconds ticked away, waiting for something—waiting for us. Where do you start with a dead baby? Do you start with CPR? Do you start with the airway? Do you start by checking its glucose? Do you start with IV access so that you can administer drugs? Do you start with checking for trauma or shaken baby syndrome? Do you start by looking for mottling of the skin to see how long it has been down? Do you start by taking its core temperature?

The answer is yes.

You start with all of these.

A young nurse next to me wrapped her hands around the baby's chest. Her thumbs started the rapid-fire compressions over the sternum, a protocol that's needed for infants. I noticed that each of her thumbnails was painted a different color. One was red; one was blue. How oddly appropriate, I thought.

The painted thumbnails moved up and down together at the frantic pace of baby chest compressions. One-two, three-four, five-six, seven-eight, nine-ten. The nurse counted out loud with each little squeeze. "One-two, three-four, five-six, seven-eight, nine-ten," she said, her voice clear and strong.

There is no specific medical reason or required protocol to count aloud. No reason except it gives you a number to hold on to instead of a thought in your head. The nurse was pregnant. I tried not to think about what it must have been like for her to give CPR to a dead baby in front of her while carrying a live baby inside of her. But she was a professional. Her face was focused. She did not shy away. The numbers rolled off her tongue.

"One-two, three-four, five-six, seven-eight, nine-ten."

Babies are born to survive in spite of arriving into a hostile world. They are the end product of evolution, evolved specifically to live in a world filled with predators. Predators like wild animals, infections, methamphetamine-addicted parents, car crashes—well, you know the rest. But like I said, they are tougher than you think. Give them a chance, and more often than not, they will find a way to hold onto life.

When an adult codes or dies suddenly, nine times out of ten it is his or her heart that has failed. On the other hand, when a baby codes, nine times out of ten, it is his or her airway that has failed. The airway is the baby's ticket to oxygen, its ticket to life. The chest compressions may help circulate the blood, but without the airway and fresh oxygen mixing in, blood is just another liquid to drown organs in.

I looked in the baby's mouth. He had no teeth, just like the woman, but his gums were shiny and pink, though dusky. There was no obstruction that I could see.

I looked up at the woman. She stood back under the crucifix hanging above the door. She had her arms crisscrossed over her chest and a hand on each shoulder, as if she were hugging herself. In the bright white light of Trauma Room Two, I could see hundreds of little craters filled with scabs, covering every inch of her arms.

She wore a black T-shirt that hung loosely on her cachectic frame. On the front of the shirt was a picture of Yosemite Sam. He held two guns in the air. Only these were not guns—they were syringes. The words across the bottom were faded and wrinkled where the white iron-on vinyl had cracked, but I could still read them: "You *meth* with the best, you die like the *rest*." Yosemite Sam was smiling. The woman was not.

"What happened?" I asked.

She paced back and forth, her arms gesturing wildly, a blur of motion. I recognized the hyper motor activity of a methamphetamine-fueled brain, increased even more by surging adrenaline. I could see on her face that she was thinking a million thoughts a second. This experience must have felt like an eternity for her. No wonder they call it speed.

"I don't know—I do not! I do not!" She repeated herself as the needle in her brain skipped on the record. She recognized her words were not quite right. She held her hands an inch in front of her face, never touching her palms to her cheeks. Her fingers suddenly wiggled and danced on the skin of her face like little suction cups on the underside of a meth-fueled starfish searching desperately for food on the bottom of the sea. It would have been wonderful if it were not so terrible.

"Does he have any medical problems? Was he a term baby? Has he even seen a doctor since he was born?" As I spoke, my hands moved as quickly as hers did. But my hands had a purpose. They flipped, snapped, and clicked together the cold steel of the laryngoscope. The light on the end beamed out, ready for action.

My questions agitated her more. "I don't know!" she screamed. "I don't know! I don't know!" She ripped out a clump of her own hair as if for emphasis. For some reason, her hand was sticky, and the hair clung to her palm. This sent her completely over the edge. She flailed her hand about, trying to shake off the clump of hair stuck to her palm, as if it were a scorpion burying its stinger into the soft flesh of her hand over and over.

She seemed to have forgotten that she had another hand with which she could have just grabbed it. She ran backward from her own hand, tripping over the stool on the side of the room. She crashed to the floor, knocking over the stool and the tray next to the bed. Little bottles of medication flew into the air, like a hive of glass bees kicked on a summer's day.

She sprang back up from the ground and into a standing position. Long brown hair dangled off her palm. She saw the dead baby and remembered why she was there. She froze in terror. I wanted to scream, *"You have killed a baby with your drug-fueled rampage! You, with your Yosemite Sam T-shirt!"* But I didn't. I had work to do.

I slipped the laryngoscope blade into the baby's mouth and lifted the tongue. I sighted down the blade. A tiny yellow-and-red plastic bead lit up; it was jammed between the vocal cords, perfectly blocking the oxygen and killing the baby.

"This infant has an airway obstruction," I heard myself say out loud.

I grabbed the size-four endotracheal tube—the tube made for baby airways—out of the airway kit. This tube is eight inches long and a little bigger in diameter than a pencil. It is clear plastic. One end is made to attach to a ventilator. The other end is beveled just slightly to help it slip between vocal cords. Once it is in place, it can blow fresh air into lungs and let the used-up air back out.

I focused on the task at hand, becoming oblivious to everything around me. Nothing in the world existed for me except the little bead stuck between the cords. All my years of training. All my sleepless nights. Everything about who I am, what I do, and why I do it was tied to this tiny little plastic bead, smaller even than the tip of my pinky.

I held the laryngoscope in my left hand. I grasped the endotracheal tube between the index and thumb in my right hand, like a pencil. I brought just the tip of it into my field of view. I took its beveled end, and I gently pushed it just to the side of the bead.

Pop.

The tiny yellow-and-red bead came out. I used the suction and took it away. It was gone. The airway was open.

I stood back up, grabbed the purple Ambu bag, and placed the oxygen mask over the baby's mouth. I squeezed the bag, which pushed the air and began to fill the blood with oxygen. The nurse squeezed his chest, which pumped the blood and sent it on its way through his body.

As the blood pumped, I imagined tiny hemoglobin soldiers running as fast as they could with fresh oxygen molecules strapped to their backs. They leaped over other cells, slid through corners, and dived into starving, dying, perishing organs with their critical supplies.

The nurse pumped away at the sternum with her thumbs. She was still counting out loud, her face a deep scowl of concentration. I could tell this baby would not die—not on her watch.

One-two, three-four, five-six, seven-eight, nine-ten.

Then something beautiful happened. The little gray baby turned pink. Pink. The color of oxygenated blood. Pink. The color of life. Pink.

The color of the sun roaring up over the mountains, bringing heat and warmth to those stranded in the snow, far from the ones they love.

Pink.

We bagged him for a minute more.

"Hold compressions," I said.

I checked for a pulse on his neck.

The nurse lifted her thumbs but kept her hands in place just in case. Her thumbs crossed, one on top of the other, just above the baby. The little chest started to move just as I felt a pulse.

He was breathing!

He panted for a moment.

The little arms and legs began to wiggle and squirm. His mouth opened wide, and he sucked in a huge breath of air before crying out with a lusty baby's roar to let the world know, *"I am still here!"*

There is no sweeter sound to my ears.

I knew this baby would live.

The big glass door of Trauma Room Two crashed open with a horrendous bang, interrupting all of us. It knocked over two chairs before smashing up against the wall.

A woman stood in the doorway scanning the room frantically. She, like the other woman, seemed to be in her twenties. But she was wearing a Taco Garden waitress outfit. Little yellow-and-red beads were decoratively pinned to her green server apron, just above her name tag on the right side of her chest.

She saw the baby and ran to him. She picked him up and pulled his little face against hers. She sobbed while he screamed his delight at being alive. His fat little arms and legs wiggled with the mad energy of life.

The woman rocked the baby back and forth in her arms. The skin of her arms was smooth, pink, clean, and healthy. "It's OK," she said. "Mommy's here now. It's OK."

The mother turned to the Yosemite Sam woman. The methed-out woman stood back, twitching, jerking, unable to stand still. Her facial muscles contracted erratically. The hair still hung from her palm, but she met the mother's gaze.

"You saved my baby; you saved my baby." The mother walked over to the woman with the scab-covered arms. Tears streamed down the mother's face. She held out her boy.

"Hold him—hold him. You saved him."

The mother turned to me. "He was choking. I was in the parking lot at work. My keys were locked in my car. This woman"—she nodded to the woman with the pockmarked arms across from her—"this woman was next to me in a car, a green Chevy Nova, just sitting there with her friends. I didn't know what to do." She started to sob. "But she did. This woman, this beautiful woman"—she pointed again at the addict—"she grabbed my baby and her friends raced him here in their car. They did not even wait for me to get in," she wiped a tear away, "but that's OK. That's OK. They did it for him. She did it for him. She saved my baby."

I watched as she handed her baby to the druggie.

The woman in the black Yosemite Sam T-shirt took the baby and held him gently in her destroyed arms. She could not stand still. Her legs still danced about, just like the baby's, but her arms cradled the child lovingly, as if he were her own.

A light appeared in her eyes.

She stood still.

She looked down at the tiny boy and smiled a toothless smile.

The baby boy smiled a toothless smile back.

And then I knew.

Knew she was a hero, a life giver, an advocate, a vanquisher, an ally, a vindicator, a patron, a champion, a defender of life, a beloved, a favorite, a superstar.

She was—what we in the business call—a Savior.

Status Epilepticus

The girl seizes.

Her body torques, twists, and jerks about, like a snake trapped on an electric fence. She flops back and forth on the gurney before us, her pale forehead dripping with sweat and her brown hair wetted black from the effort of muscle contractions that threaten to tear her tiny frame apart.

Trauma Room Two is silent, save for the *gluck-gluck-gluck* of her gagging as jaw and teeth grind and bang together, out of control. This. Is. Seizure. Her body screams with each shimmy and shake.

Her father stands next to me. He strokes her head with trembling fingers, running them through her damp hair and trying to keep the strands out of her grimacing face. His fingers move in time with the rhythmic nod of her skull as the tonic-clonic seizure ratchets and cranks her body. I take a deep breath. I start my chant.

"Break, seizure, break."

"Break, seizure, break."

I say it in my head, I say it in my bones, I say it in every part of me, keeping time to her dance.

"Break, seizure, break."

I need to stall. I need to wait. I need to ride this out. The medicine will work. I just have to give it a little more time.

I look over at her father standing next to me as he gazes down at his thirteen-year-old daughter. Written across his face is a sadness so deep, so dark, and so complete that even I can feel it in my deadened chest. Its claws jerk and tear away at me with each awful buck of her body.

"Break, seizure, break."

"Break, seizure, break."

I repeat it in my mind. Again. And again. And again.

Her skin turns a pasty gray as her oxygen level falls. Her brain is forgetting how to breathe. If I give her sedation and put a tube down her trachea to breathe for her, I will not know whether she is seizing. But if I do not, well, she may just stop breathing forever. It's a catch-22, a rock and a hard place, a lose-lose bet with a stacked deck in the casino of the *Titanic* as it careens into an iceberg.

But choose I must.

Her dad watches, petting her head, waiting. I know she has had bad seizures before when I see how calmly he sits with his sadness, watching his only daughter disappear in front of him. He does not panic, and he does not cry out; he, too, has seen hundreds, maybe thousands, of seizures—maybe even more than I. But unlike me, each one takes another piece of his daughter. They carry her away, little by little, to that other place out beyond the horizon that we cannot reach.

"Break, seizure, break."

"Break, seizure, break."

My gut begins to twist. My breath becomes shallow. My hands begin to shake. Maybe this is the one that will never stop. Maybe this is the campfire that precedes the forest fire that burns down all that stands in its path. I know I have to stop it now, or it will burn through this girl, leaving nothing behind but a smoldering empty shell.

I look up at the clock. The green digital numbers stand unchanging, as if painted onto the wall. I have four medications dripping into her arms as fast as they can go. I have given round after round of drugs through the IV, trying to extinguish these roaring flames before me.

The clock states indifferently that it has only been one minute since her last dose. One sixty-second burst of time. One little tiny slice of a slice of a slice. Time respects no one inside Trauma Room Two.

I have to ride it out a little longer.

I look at her mom. She stands back with a blank look on her face. I know that look. She must have been drained and drained, seizure after seizure, until finally, one day, there was nothing left to drain. She looks to have departed somewhere else. I can't say I blame her. A person can only spill so much sadness before he or she runs dry.

"Break, seizure, break."

"Break, seizure, break."

The digit on the clock finally changes to a new number. It has now been two minutes. She is dusky, almost blue. I draw up another dose of medication, ready to fire. I tear open the intubation equipment, ready to dash into the house before it burns to the ground.

But the seizure breaks. The fire has run out of fuel. All movement stops. The absence of her shaking suddenly feels unbearably loud. I notice the monitor again, beeping along with her racing heart. I know her breath is coming.

Just wait.

Wait.

Wait.

Her oxygen levels fall further, triggering another alarm on the monitor. The alarms now call back and forth like two panicked, drowning dogs. No one moves in Trauma Room Two, though the air fills with a cacophony of the alarms' almost unbearable cries.

I see her mom. She stares blankly ahead, oblivious to the noise. It occurs to me that maybe she is making a mental grocery list for later. Maybe she is trying to remember whether it was Tuesday or Wednesday when she last went to the store. Or maybe she is not thinking at all; maybe she is just empty.

The ER nurse across from me makes eye contact. We look at each other. She knows what I know. Wait. We nod to each other subtly, trying to encourage the other. The breath will come.

I look back at her dad. He stares at his daughter, trying to will her to breathe even though he knows by now he has no power over any of this. But try he does. I see it in his face. He has not been drained all the way—not yet, at least. Life is drilling him full of holes as fast as it can, adding another big one today. I see he does not shy away from the horror like most. He is going to fight this to the bitter end, no matter the cost to himself, his sanity, or his soul.

A desperate gasp bursts forth from the girl, interrupting my thoughts. It is followed by another. And then another. Her brain is remembering to breathe. Her oxygen level rises, her skin pinks up, and she starts to move. The medicine or the chant worked; I never know which one does what anymore.

She opens her eyes. She sees her mom. Mom gives a little smile, but her daughter's eyes stay blank. They jerk around erratically, looking for something—someone. They see me, the nurse, the room, the alarms, and the monitors, all of which she holds her eyes to for a second as her brain struggles to understand what she sees…"No, *not this, not this, not this.*"

She sees her dad. Her eyes stop. He is crying, as he must have done ten thousand times before and will do another ten thousand times more. I watch as her eyes stay fixed on her father's face like a distant beacon through the fog in her head. Little by little she guides herself back by his steady light. We all watch as his daughter starts to return before us, the snake that possessed her slithering away, back to some dark, faraway place where it will stay until next time.

She stares at her father. And then it clicks—who he is and why he is crying. She smiles a gentle smile at him. He takes her hand.

In that brief moment, I see why he fights so hard.

At least five seizures a night, every night, for eight years, they tell me. They came out of nowhere. No family history, and no medical problems. They just started one day, and they have not stopped since. Every test, every drug has been tried, and then tried again. Every specialist has been visited, and then visited again. They've been told that there are no specialists left to see or drugs left to try.

I put a hand on her father's shoulder and stand there, feeling somehow unworthy to be in the presence of such a raw, exposed soul. I know only too well that in this business, it is foolish to hope, but I find myself saying a quiet prayer to some God I once knew...

"Just this once."

"Just this once."

"Save this one."

Family

They found him in the ditch. He lay tucked behind the bushes. A brown frayed tarp held together with strands of silver duct tape covered him completely. At first the jogger who found him thought he had discovered a dead body, but then the tarp moved, cursed at the runner's dog, and wiggled back down farther into the bushes.

The jogger called 9-1-1. The police came. They tried to stand him up, but he was too drunk. They in turn called the medics. The medics came. After a few minutes of watching him stumble about, they loaded the man into their ambulance to bring him once again to our ER.

I was standing at the nurse's station when I heard the call come in over the radio. The medics said they were bringing in an intoxicated transient found down by Shots Creek. It was all I could do not to run to the radio and demand they put him back where they had found him.

But by then it was too late.

I heard the sirens.

He was back.

The medics wheel him in through the big ambulance bay door. He sits up on the gurney as the medics push it. When he sees the staff of the emergency room glaring at him, he smiles. With great drama, he waves his hand using his wrist and elbow, as if he is the star attraction on a float in a homecoming parade. Angry grumbles fill the air. I shake my head with disgust. He sees me staring and gives me an extra big, toothless smile. It is clear he is loving every second of this.

Today is the forty-second time he has been in this emergency department in the last twelve months. Not one of those times has he ever been sober. Nor does it look like he is today.

I work at the desk for a moment while the nurses check him in. After a few minutes, they flag him on the board as ready to be seen by the doctor. I try to motivate myself to go see him but it does not work. Instead, I decide to make him wait while I see every other patient in the emergency department first.

Twenty minutes later I am done seeing everyone but him. I sit back down at the computer. Unfortunately, for once, we are not that busy. There are only three patients in the ER besides him. Maybe I should just leave him unseen in the room until the next doctor comes on shift in ten hours. God knows he is still going to be here regardless of what I do.

With a sigh of resignation, I realize there is no escape. I click on his name and assign myself as the treating physician. The screen flashes to the medical record. His chief complaint today is back pain. It gives me pause; for him that is unusual. Maybe today there is actually something wrong with him.

I log out, stand up from the computer, and walk over toward room three. I pass the nurse who checked him in. She sees where I am going and smacks herself dramatically in the forehead with her palm while rolling her eyes. I suppress a laugh, at least we are all in this together.

I step into the room. The lights are low. He is asleep. Today he wears a faded black baseball cap. In pale yellow letters the words "Vietnam Veteran" are spelled out across the front and then again along the left top of the bill. A series of tiny, colored military flags are embroidered in between the words "Vietnam" and "Veteran."

The cap holds down a head of frizzy brown hair. It grows everywhere, spilling out from under the cap and stretching across his face, shoulders, and chest as if someone has dumped a bucket of scraggly weeds onto his head. He is a mess. By the smell of him, I can tell he has not had a shower in a very long time.

I give a little cough to let him know I am here. He snores away, oblivious. I shake the bed rail. He mumbles something about a dog and scratches his beard. A green leaf the size of a child's thumbnail drops onto the sheets next to him.

I flip on the lights. He pulls the bill of the cap down over his eyes. In the light, I notice there are several sticks and leaves embedded in his beard from where he slept last night.

"Wake up!" I give the bed rail a less-than-gentle shake.

He rolls onto his side, putting his arm up over his face.

"Leave me alone!" he grumbles.

More foliage drops onto the sheets. He is wearing a patchy flannel shirt that is covered in burrs, seeds, and little leaves. Underneath it is a yellow sweat-stained T-shirt that clings to his chest. A pair of gray military dog tags hang down onto the shirt. One of the tags is flipped up; one is flipped down.

Maybe I should just let him sleep. I have better things to do with my time. I know what he wants, anyway. At least if he is sleeping, I know where he is in the department.

As I watch, he kicks his boots around in the bed, knocking the sheet off his legs. He has on a brand new pair of tan Carhartt pants held up with a frayed rope and tied in a square knot. I would bet you there is a clothesline somewhere in town with a missing pair of new pants.

"Wake up!" I say it again.

"I ain't bothering anybody, Doc. Let me sleep!" he snarls, kicking his legs spasmodically as if trying to swim up toward the top of the bed.

I sigh and gently lift his backpack from his side, setting it under the gurney. His name is written in shaky handwriting across the back of it with a permanent marker.

Scooter.

"Scooter!" I shout. "Scooter! Wake up!" I kick the wheel of the gurney with my heel and the whole bed shakes.

He coughs and sputters, "What's wrong you, man? Seriously?"

I take a deep breath and restrain myself from kicking the gurney even harder. I can't help but imagine how great it would feel to wheel him out into the parking lot still on the gurney and give it a big push down the hill next to the hospital. Sure, I would lose my job and license, but on the other hand, I would never, ever have to deal with Scooter again. I know I sound uncaring, but after twelve months of this, Scooter has more than used up my patience.

It all started about a year ago when he first showed up in town. Like most drifters, the first thing he did when he arrived was head straight to the emergency department. Everyone who lives on the road, it seems, always wants to know what the ER is like in a new town.

Is it hard to get pain pills or easy? What are the security guards like? Will security kick you off campus for sitting in the waiting room on a rainy day? Will they kick you out on a sunny day? Each town and ER is different, and I suppose that is part of what makes living on the road so appealing to some people.

But Scooter was different from most drifters. When he showed up, he stood in line at the desk. He did not have any physical complaints at all. In fact, all he asked for was an application. An application to be a volunteer in the ER.

No one had the slightest idea of what to do. This had never happened before. Sure, we had a few volunteers, but they were always either high school kids with big dreams of becoming doctors or eighty-year-old Rotary Club women who liked to chat. We definitely had never had a toothless, homeless, drunk volunteer.

Ms. Dower out at the front desk reportedly tried to tell him we were not hiring. Scooter quickly pointed out that it was not a paid position— it was a volunteer position. The two of them went round and round for several minutes before the secretary finally gave up and handed him an application. He filled it out and turned it in, and off it went.

Twice his application went up and then back down the chain of administration before the answer came back. No. He could not volunteer unless he was clean and sober. That was non-negotiable.

Scooter begged and pleaded and even cried a little bit. So we made a deal with him. We would *maybe* consider him for the position if he went to detox and got cleaned up. He wanted us to guarantee him that he would get the spot when he returned. We made it very clear that was not how things worked around here. In the end, he agreed. So we set him up for detox, and off he went.

Three weeks later he was back. He stayed sober just long enough to fill out another application. The next day he did not show up for the interview. I had one of the medics walk down under the bridge by the river, and she found him passed out with a bottle of vodka. Well, that's the end of that, we all thought.

But it wasn't.

A couple of days later, Scooter returned again. This time he had on a new shirt he had clearly borrowed from another clothesline. It was ridiculously large on him, but he was trying. He filled out the same application, promised that he really wanted detox and to work in the ER, and, well, once again was loaded up in the back of an ambulance and sent off. This time he only made it a week. Word reached us he was kicked out for sneaking in some booze.

After that he stopped trying to apply for a volunteer position. Instead, he got it into his confused head that he should apply for a paid position. Scooter applied for a job as ER security. For past work experience, he listed "army guy."

So of course administration met again. No one wanted to be seen as prejudiced against the homeless man or an army vet—if he actually was one—but very quickly the answer came back again: no. For the same reason. Either he was sober, or it was a no go. So once again, we loaded him up in another ambulance and sent him off.

I know this sounds ridiculous. But I am not making this up. I swear.

This time he only made it two days in detox before he signed out early and returned to his place under the bridge. For a couple of weeks, Scooter tried to get other positions in the ER. Housekeeping, supply—you name it. He just kept trying but our answer was the same. No. Go away. Do not come back until you are sober. Or just go away. We have a busy ER to run.

For a while Scooter resigned himself to hanging out in our waiting room. But enough patients complained about the Unabomber look-alike stumbling around that eventually we had to do something.

Administration had its final and last meeting. Scooter was banned from campus unless he was a patient. Somehow I ended up being the one who had to sit down with him and explain the situation. He cried the whole time, big drunk tears rolling down his face and disappearing into his beard.

That was the end of his trying to work with us.

That was three months ago.

"Scooter!" I shake his big toe where it sticks out through the hole in the end of his boot.

"Scooter! Wake up! I got things to do!"

He pulls the sheet up over his head to hide, as if it were his own personal tarp.

"Leave me alone, Doc!"

"I can't leave you alone. You are in the emergency room. You are a patient."

He is quiet.

"Did you hurt your back?" I ask.

He mumbles something I can't understand.

"What?" I ask, losing my temper.

He mumbles again.

"Take down the sheet, and talk to me like an adult, or I am going to tell the nurses to lock you in the psych room again." I rub the muscles in my neck, trying not to tense up.

"Did you hurt your back or not?"

At those words he suddenly flips down the sheet and looks at me with a big grin.

"I am suicidal…" he says, delighted that he got me to ask about his back.

I groan.

"Dammit, Scooter, we have real patients here. I don't have time for games."

"I'm suicidal, Doc. I just know if you release me, I am going to kill myself."

It is the exact same thing he always says.

By stating he is suicidal, he has just bought himself a bed in the ER until a crisis worker can see him. It is the law in this state.

To a man who lives under a tarp, it is a wonderful law. With those three words, he has just bought himself, at the very least, three hot meals and a clean bed for the day. Three hots and a cot, we call it.

To an ER doctor, it is a terrible law. It means we have to feed him, listen to him complain about pretty much everything, and have him hang out in the ER until a crisis worker can drive to our town and evaluate him.

If he would just lie quietly in his bed like most patients, it would not be so bad. But this is Scooter we are talking about. Some drunk part of his brain has recently started to believe he is on staff here and part of our ER family. If we leave him unattended for long, he will sneak out of his room and start trying to resupply towels, stack up boxes in back, bring patients cups of water or coffee, and otherwise do things that a drunk, homeless person should never do in an ER.

A couple of times, he has even put on a stethoscope and wandered into a patient's room, introducing himself as the doctor. It would be hilarious if I were not the one who got the complaint letters from patients and their families.

"*Su-i-cidal…*" He says it again, rolling it off his tongue with delight. He leans back in bed and interlaces his fingers behind his head. He crosses his boots and lets out a relaxed sigh as if he has just disembarked from a long flight to the tropics and finally, after twelve hours of travel, arrived at the beach. With great drama, as I watch, he punches the nurse call button.

"Can I help you?" I hear our secretary's voice.

"This is Scooter." He claps his hands and rubs them together for emphasis. "What's on the menu today?" he says to the little speaker.

I hear a groan from our secretary.

He looks up from the button with a twinkle in his eyes.

"I'm starving."

I throw my hands up in disgust and leave.

I honestly don't know what to do with him. I won't say who, exactly, but a little while ago, a doctor and some nurses got together and bought a one-way bus ticket to New Orleans. It was offered free of charge to Scooter with a gift certificate for a free steak dinner at the nicest restaurant in New Orleans once he arrived. It seemed like a good idea at the time.

When we gave it to him, he started crying his big drunk tears again. He tore it up. He said that was the nicest thing anyone had ever done for him and that there was no way he could leave such a loving family. Several nurses present explained with a string of expletives that he was not part of this family. But Scooter did not hear a word they said.

I finally—I mean, the ER doctor who bought the bus ticket—had to pull the nurses away from him and remind them that nothing good would come from strangling a homeless drunk.

The radio buzzes in the ER, pulling me back to the present, as I step out into the hall. It is time to start the long process of getting Scooter medically cleared for a psych eval. They will want blood work, drug screens, and a blood-alcohol level back before they will even consider seeing him. That will take two hours before those tests are back. Then his blood-alcohol level has to be low enough for them to see him.

Scooter lives intoxicated. That means his blood-alcohol level is never low. So we have to wait until he gets the shakes; we give him alcohol-withdrawal medicine hour after hour, and finally when it is low enough, we call the crisis worker. The worker then informs us how many patients are ahead of Scooter, but that, when he gets a chance, he will get in his car and start the drive down here. More than once I have thought we should just give up and get Scooter his own permanent room here.

Oh well—no use wasting any more time thinking about Scooter. A new patient has checked in. Back to work.

I sign up for the next patient. It is a man named Davis. He, too, has checked in with back pain. I skim through the chart for Davis. There is not much. There is a post office box in California listed as his last address. It says "homeless" under current residence. I wonder briefly if Scooter knows him. I keep reading. No past medical history. Twenty-eight years old. Chief complaint is chronic back pain; no acute injury. Out of pain pills and wants a refill.

In a small town ER, you get to know who is from your town and who is not. Occasionally we get people from out of town whom we have never seen before. People who clearly do not belong. People who are looking for drugs, trouble, or both.

For some reason they have put him in Trauma Room Two while they repair the faucet in room six. No matter. I step into the room. Immediately alarm bells go off in my head.

A big man sits cross-legged on the bed. His head is shaved and shiny. Laced black military-style boots run up over his ankles. When he sees me, he twists from side to side stretching his back as far as it will go. He twists so hard the joints audibly *pop-pop-pop*, and the blood vessels on both sides of his head bulge from effort. He grins.

He is wearing black cargo pants and a red TapouT T-shirt. It is skin tight against oversize pecs and biceps. As he twists in bed, the muscles of his arms ball up grossly. Either he is a world-class weight lifter, or he is a serious steroid abuser. I am guessing the second.

He has three teardrop-shaped tattoos just beneath the corner of his left eye. His nose has two slight crooks midway down, where it has been broken more than once. Small linear scars are sprinkled over a prominent forehead and cheekbones. They are the scars of a street fighter. His neck is huge and grotesquely muscled with a purple spider web tattoo across it. A little black spider tattoo the size of a dime hangs suspended from a lone thread down over his Adam's apple—so that each time he swallows, the spider bobs on the web. It is nasty.

"Busy today, Doc?" He extends a hand. I notice he has the letters *G-O-D-S* tattooed on the knuckles of his right hand. I catch a glimpse of his other hand. The letters *W-I-L-L* are tattooed across it. His fists together read: "GODS WILL." Nice.

"Not too busy yet." I shake his hand, and he squeezes it overly hard, trying to make me flinch. He smiles and looks right at me. It is a challenge of sorts for what is coming.

We both know it.

There is a commotion in the hall, and I hear someone yelling at Scooter. We both glance out the glass door at the same time to see a nurse take Scooter by the arm back to his room.

Davis laughs.

I turn back to him.

"How can I help you today?" I ask him.

"You tell me—you're the doctor." He gives a feral grin as if to display his cleverness.

I stand staring at him, ignoring his jest, my face blank. He lets go of my hand.

This, too, is the dance of the ER doctor.

Silence hangs between us for a good twenty seconds. I am conscious of several facts that he may or may not be aware of. One, I am between him and the door. Two, his hands are where I can see them. Three, his legs are still crossed where he sits on the bed.

"How can I help you?" I ask again.

"Well, Doc-dur," he says, "I hurt my back a couple years ago in the military. I was Special Forces." He stares at me, daring me to challenge his story.

I do not.

"I broke six bones in my lower spine jumping out of a plane. I've had three operations on it since. I'm half metal, Doc." He guffaws at his own tired joke. His face turns serious. "I have an extremely high tolerance for pain. One of the highest they have ever seen in the army." He cracks his knuckles for emphasis. "But my back injury is so bad it is only bearable with high dose pain meds. The pain would probably kill a normal man."

He pauses again, staring at my face. I can feel him trying to read me to figure out how he is going to hook me into his story.

I empty my face and body language of all possible meaning, as I have learned to do.

He continues. "My regular doctor is in California. My meds got stolen on the bus ride up here." He swings his legs down and hangs them over the side of the bed. I move back just a tiny bit.

"I called my doctor, and he said to go to the ER right away and get my pain meds. Before it gets out of control." He twists again from side to side, cracking his back as he does so. I am tempted to point out that he moves his back extremely well for someone in so much pain. But I am not an idiot.

"When it gets bad, I have problems with my temper." He smiles again, but it is not so much a smile as it is a showing of teeth.

I stay completely blank. In a consciously bored and neutral tone, I ask, "Where does it hurt?" I step over to the bed to examine his back. He leans away from me suddenly and puts his hands up as if telling me to stop.

"Whoa, I don't like how you approach me. You're a little aggressive there, Doc-dur," he says and challenges me again with his eyes.

This, too, is part of the game. He wants me to respond. He wants to engage me, to argue with me, to dare me to challenge him so that he can intimidate me with his size. I know this game. It may be new to him, but it is an old one to me.

I ignore his comment, pretending not to understand.

"Do you want me to examine your back or not?" I ask in a flat tone.

He pauses for a moment and then nods. "That's why I'm here."

I barely touch the skin of his lower back when he cries out in severe pain. "Oh God, oh God, you triggered a spasm!" He flops back violently in bed and begins rolling back and forth, cussing extremely loudly. I would laugh at how pathetic his acting is, but I know this is not a game to him.

To him this is a hunt.

I stand there unmoving, as if I don't understand what is happening. I play dumb. I have to be extremely careful. The slightest eye roll or sigh, and I know he will be in my face. I can see some steroid-fueled monster lurks just underneath the surface. All it takes is one wrong word on my part and that monster will be released.

After a moment, he stops writhing. "I need pain meds, Doc. I need pain meds real bad. I have five broken bones in my back. Five." He holds up five fingers. I notice he has silver rings on each one.

He can't even keep his story straight. A minute ago it was six broken bones. Or maybe he is daring me to point out the inconsistency so that we can argue.

"They are going to do surgery again; I'm just waiting for my insurance to approve it."

"Is that through the VA?" I ask.

He stares confused for a second but catches on quickly. "Yeah, yeah, it's through the VA. It's part of my benefits from the military." He scrambles to cover for his slip-up, but it is too late. That moment of hesitation tells me all I need to know.

He senses now that he has somehow messed up, which seems to just make him angrier. "I can't handle the pain." He white knuckles the bed rails for emphasis. "It makes me go crazy. The pain makes me go crazy."

I step back, increasing the space between us again. This is not going to end well. I am tempted to just give him some pain pills and be done with it. But I have learned, as every ER doc learns, that if you do that, they will be back the next day demanding more—and the next day and the day after that.

You have to stop them the first time.

Don't get me wrong. If I thought he had a real medical problem, I would give him pain meds in a second. But I don't. I think he is lying through his teeth to me.

I point to the sign about pain meds on the wall, and in the most boring, bureaucratic voice I can muster, I explain our narcotic-pain-medication policy, ending with "we do not refill lost prescriptions for narcotics." In my head, I think, *Especially for people who show up from out of town wanting pain meds.*

Just as I finish I hear the voice of the hospital operator overhead. "Security to the ER. Security to the ER." I look around confused. I am doing fine; I don't need security with this guy. Then I realize it has to be Scooter.

The call for security overhead agitates the fire in Davis like an infusion of gasoline. He glares at the speakers on the ceiling and then back at me.

"You calling security on me, Doc?"

He tenses his pecs and shoulders, puffing up his chest. He reminds me of a dog getting ready to fight. He clenches and unclenches his fists. If he knew our security guard was a sixty-year-old retired janitor, he might not be so upset. Regardless, I add it to the list of Scooter's offenses. Next time he shows up, I am just locking him in the psych room right away and being done with it.

Davis sits back suddenly, shifting tactics again. "No problem, Doc. No problem. I'm not looking for trouble, just some help." He grins again. He is suddenly my best friend. "You live here in town, Doc? Got a pretty wife and some little kids?"

Ah, the friendly veiled threat. This guy has been around to a lot of ERs. He is trying every trick, every tactic, to get under my skin.

"Which bones are broken in your back?" I ask, ignoring his question.

He frowns. He is still scrambling.

"It happened when I served in the military," he repeats.

"Which bones are broken in your back?" I state again, more slowly.

It dawns on him that he is not getting any pain meds out of me. He can see it. The decision has been made. I don't hide it.

He stands up, looming over me.

"You ever been in the military?" he asks.

"No."

"Well, I served people like you. I put my life on the line. And the only thanks I got was a broken back and a bunch of asshole doctors refusing to give me pain meds."

He takes a step toward me.

He pulls up his shirt to reveal a perfect six-pack of muscles. A tattoo of Jesus dying on the cross is tattooed upside down across his abdomen. He turns sideways and punches a fist into his own right kidney. "It's right there. The pain is right there, Doc." His eyes go wide with anger. He punches himself again. "That's what it feels like." He punches again even harder, leaving a red mark on his skin. I can't help but notice all the supposed surgeries that he's had have left not a single scar.

"You want me to just stay in pain? Is that it?" He glares at me. "Here—put your hand on it."

I step back but not quickly enough.

He grabs my hand by the wrist. "Here, Doc. You wanna know what it feels like?"

I try to pull my hand away, but I can't. I am trapped. We both stand there, me trying to pull my hand away, him with his giant fingers pressing into my wrist.

I hear something behind me. "You got a problem, Doc?" I turn around. It's Scooter. He is standing in the doorway, swaying slightly from side to side. His black Vietnam hat has halfway fallen off his head. He tucks his dog tags into his shirt.

"No, Scooter, everything is fine. Go back to your room."

Scooter stands there for a minute, looking back and forth, from Davis to me. My hand is still trapped in his. No one moves. I can see the drunk wheels spinning in Scooter's head, as he is trying to make sense of it.

Finally, Davis speaks slowly, almost in a whisper. "Yeah, Scooter, go back to your room before you get hurt."

Before I can react, Scooter leaps forward and grabs Davis's wrist, twisting it away from mine into some sort of joint lock. With his other hand, he pushes Davis back, pinning him to the wall, driving the little spider on his neck back against his throat, crushed by Scooter's thumb.

I freeze, afraid to move.

Scooter twists harder, and I hear the pop of a finger joint being dislocated. Davis goes weak at the knees and tries to collapse, but Scooter keeps him pushed against the wall with his thumb digging into the front of the man's giant neck.

"Scooter!" I start to say.

Scooter leans in and whispers to Davis something I can't hear. The giant man's face turns sheet white, and he looks like he is going to cry. It is quite a transformation from the monster who was here just a moment ago.

The man begins to choke and gag, and for a moment, I am afraid Scooter is going to kill him. But at the last second Scooter drops his hands and steps back. Davis falls to his knees, coughing and gagging, and I notice his middle finger has been dislocated.

Without a word, he stands up and runs out of the room like a child who has just been spanked.

Scooter turns around with a sheepish look on his face.

"I was in the army once." He shrugs. He pulls his dog tags back out of his T-shirt collar.

"I believe it," I answer.

Our old security guard comes huffing and puffing into the room. He sees Scooter, and he shakes his head. He turns to me and asks, "Scooter giving you problems again, Doc?"

I look at Scooter.

"Who, Scooter?" I put my arm over his shoulders. "Nah, he's never a problem; he's one of us."

———

It turns out sometimes all a person needs is a chance to prove himself.

So if you happen to see a security guard (six months sober, by the way) with no teeth and a big beard, well, one, listen to him when he tells you to sit down, and two, leave him alone—he's family.

Hands

I watch her die.

She is eighty-six years old, two months, twenty-three days, four hours, six minutes, and nineteen seconds. No, make that twenty seconds now.

I stand next to the bed in Trauma Room Two. Someone has left on the giant overhead light that hangs down from the ceiling on a swing arm for traumas. Its blinding beam shines like the world's brightest spotlight on the bed. In the middle of the light sits a woman, one hand on her belly, the other hand just above her eyes as she tries to block out the glare.

"Sorry," I say.

I reach up and click off the light. I blink several times, my eyes readjusting.

She ignores me, swaying slightly. I notice she has long straight hair that reaches past bony shoulders to her waist. With each little sway of her torso a few strands of her hair float a half second behind. They look like lone threads of silk carried on the wind. The rest of her hair is silver and white and vibrant. Can a dying woman have hair that is vibrant? *"Well,"* I think to myself, *"I guess she can."*

I glance up at the monitor. Blood pressure is eighty-three over forty now. That is too low. She already has two large-bore IVs started by the medics. Both IV machines are pumping at full speed, their electric hum and buzz audible in the quiet room. Bilateral streams of saline drip into clear plastic tubing that runs into her arms. The fluids flow into her blood vessels. They pour in just as fast as the blood pours out. Out into her abdominal cavity from her leaking aneurysm.

The aneurysm is in her aorta, the biggest blood vessel in her body. It carries the blood like a living pipeline from the heart down through the thorax and into the abdomen. Eventually, it splits into the smaller femoral arteries. Her aneurysm sits just above the split, right on one of the largest parts of the vessel.

With each beat of her heart, blood is sent gushing through it. Eighty-six years of high blood pressure has taken its toll on the piping. It is stretching like a balloon now, tearing further with each beat, leaking and spilling, thinning and ripping, getting ready to burst.

When it goes, she goes.

I stand with an ultrasound probe in my hand. There is bluish ultrasound jelly smeared across the pale skin of her distended stomach. Ten seconds ago I saw it. I put the probe on her belly and saw the big black balloon inside that means only one thing.

"You have a rupturing aneurysm in your belly." I take a breath, looking up from the screen. "You are going to die if you do not have surgery immediately."

Those are my exact words. Surgery or death. Even if she chooses surgery, she may still die, but at least she will die with a chance. Without surgery, the only guarantee is death.

Sometimes this job is nothing more than simply presenting people with a choice.

Today it is her turn to choose.

She needs to decide, and she needs to decide right now. She cannot wait. Each second she hesitates decreases the chance she will survive the operating room.

I notice she still rests her left hand on the side of her abdomen—I am guessing because it hurts. She wears a silver ring that displays a small diamond and one ruby on either side. One spot is empty; one of the rubies has fallen out, and it has not been replaced. I wonder briefly what has become of it. Surely she has noticed it. Maybe she thought later she would have it fixed. Only now there is no later.

This is it.

I can see her hand on her belly bounce ever so slightly with each beat of her heart. For some reason I think of a pregnant woman feeling for the kick of an unborn child. I bet she can feel the kick of her aorta stretching with each beat of her heart, like a little foot kicking against her hand. Only this gestation will birth an end, not a beginning. At my words, her hand slides down to her side, and I can see she suddenly is no longer so curious about what it is kicking away in her belly.

I keep waiting for her to nod. To say out loud, "Yes, help me. It hurts." She just needs to say it. I am ready to run from the room for the phone to call the surgeon. It is a true emergency. Her aneurysm is a bomb that, when it finally detonates, cannot be undone.

Only she does not answer for a moment. I squeeze the rail, waiting. I start to feel light-headed before realizing that I am holding my breath. I exhale slowly and try to force myself to relax. It is funny, in an odd sort of way, that this affects me so strongly. It is not my life that hangs in the balance. Whether she lives or dies, I will be fine. Yet my heart bangs away in my chest as if my life, too, hangs on her decision.

She still does not speak. Instead, she flicks a few rebellious strands of hair out of her face with her left hand. Her eyes lose focus for a moment. She looks into the distance. *"What is she thinking?"* I wonder. More seconds pass. I clear my throat, not wanting to pressure her, but, hey, the clock is ticking.

She blinks a few times and I can tell she has made a decision. I lean forward. She looks up at me and then does something that surprises me.

She smiles.

In spite of what must be awful pain, she grins at me. In that instant, I see she is a brave woman. A woman who has been unafraid to live and now, incredibly, is unafraid to die. I try to swallow, but my mouth is dry. I know what she is going to say, and it frightens me. I am not as brave as she is. Not yet.

She speaks. "If I do not have surgery and I am going to die, can you make sure it does not hurt like this?"

I pause, thinking for a second, choosing each word carefully. I want to be sure about what I say. My words are the last she will ever hear, so I want to be sure I do not deceive her in any way. I want her to die with the truth in her ears, whatever it may be.

"Yes. Yes, I can do that." I nod. "I promise you I can take away the pain. Whatever happens, it will not hurt." The ability to alleviate suffering is one small power that I do have.

She clenches her jaw for a second as a wave of pain hits her. She grabs her belly with both hands and moans. Her brow begins to glisten. And then she speaks again.

"Promise me. Promise me you will stay here next to me to make sure that it does not hurt." The pain has brought some fear into her face. Fear of the unknown. Fear of where she will be an hour from now, a day from now, a year from now. But she is brave; she keeps her wits about her even with her fear.

I run through the list of other patients in the ER in my head. A woman with abdominal pain, most likely stomach flu. A twenty-three-year-old man with tooth pain. A five-year-old girl with a fever, probably a cold. An old man with a cough. A suicidal teen. A woman with chest pain and a negative workup waiting to be discharged.

They will all have to wait. They will not like it. They will be angry with me if this takes too long. I guess they can fill out the survey the hospital will send them, and they can write about how I made them wait. I shrug. When they are ready to die, I will be there for them. It will be their turn to make the others wait.

"Yes," I say. "I promise you I will not leave your side."

She nods, her silver hair waving back and forth ever so slightly. Her face relaxes a tiny bit. "OK." She squints, gathering her courage.

She looks me in the eye. "I do not want to have surgery." She pauses and looks at me. "I am ready to die. Let's do this."

A chill runs down my spine. You would think that after fifteen years of this, it would not affect me so. But it still does.

It is strange to think I do not know her story. In fact, I do not know anything about her. She just rolled through the door on the ambulance gurney with belly pain and low blood pressure. Ten minutes ago, I had never met her, and yet now I am the one who will sit with her at her death.

"Is there anyone I can call for you?" I ask.

"Not unless this is going to take six or more hours. My kids live on the other side of the mountains."

"Do you want me to call them?" I ask anyway.

She stares at me for a moment. "No. Sit here with me. I just saw them at Thanksgiving. Let that be their last memory of me. Just tell them I went quickly."

"OK," I answer.

The nurse comes in and gives her morphine. I watch as the woman's face relaxes ever so slightly, the pain fading in the warmth of opiates.

"Do you want me to sit in here with her?" the nurse asks.

The patient looks at me. I remember my promise. "No, we are OK. I will call you if she needs more pain meds." The nurse shrugs and steps out of the room.

It is just the woman and me again.

I look up at the monitor. Her blood pressure is sixty-eight over thirty-two now. It won't be long.

She closes her eyes and leans her head back against the pillow. Again I wonder what she is thinking. What would I be thinking about if it were the last few minutes of my life? My family? My job? Would I still be so curious about what happens after our time here? I don't know. I guess I will have to wait my turn like everybody else.

We both sit quietly. The monitor beeps along with her heart. I take the moment to reflect on my life in this place. I have been so burned out lately. It seems I am just doing the same thing over and over without really doing anything at all. Staff members have been angry. My patients have been angry. Angry parents, angry spouses, angry siblings.

At times it seems that all the anger is directed at me because there is nowhere else for them to direct it. Sometimes I want to say to people, "I am not the reason you are sick." But I know it is easier for them if they just yell at me for a few moments. At least they can yell at someone. But after a while, it makes me want to quit, to walk away, and not come back. "I get sick, too," I want to say back. "I get tired, too," I want to argue. But I never do.

And then something like this happens. I look at her. She is dying now. I am the last person she will ever speak with. The last person she will ever see. The last human being on this planet for all eternity who will hear her voice, see her blink, see her swallow, hear her cough, or see her smile.

This is why I became a doctor. Not because I can stitch a wound, manage a trauma, or splint an arm.

No, I became a doctor to be with people when it matters the most. I did it so that I can stand at the edge of the cliff with another human being and we can gaze out together into the night beyond. I did it because I, too, am afraid. I did it because I want to find some way to lessen the fear—not just for me but for all of us.

She opens her eyes and creases furl her brow, a pained expression wrinkling her face.

"Are you hurting?" I ask.

She nods, embarrassed.

"I don't want you to hurt," I say. "Don't be afraid to tell me." I push the call button for her. The nurse appears.

"Ten more of morphine," I say.

The nurse nods, draws up the meds, and pushes them through the IV. I give the nurse a nod, and she leaves again. She, too, has other patients.

"Thank you," the woman says and sits back.

My hand rests on the side rail beside her. She grabs it and squeezes it tightly.

"Thank you for sitting with me."

I blush. "Sure," I say. "Sure."

"What is your name?" she asks.

"I am Dr. Green," I say out of habit.

Her eyes twinkle with amusement. "No, what is your *name*?"

It takes me a moment to understand. Sometimes I am kind of dense that way. But I figure it out eventually.

"My name is Philip."

"Hi, Philip. I am Ann." She gives my hand a little squeeze.

"Hi, Ann," I say. "It's nice to meet you." I smile as we shake hands as if we are meeting for the first and last time, which we are.

She laughs. "And it's nice to meet you."

We hold hands.

It is sad and wonderful and terrible and beautiful to hold the hand of a dying person. I look around the room. There is a ventilator with a touch screen interface, a fiber optic GlideScope, a monitor that captures every beat of her heart, her every breath, her oxygen level, and her blood pressure. There are three computers in this room alone, not including the telestroke robot used for stroke patients. It hits me that I am surrounded by nearly as much technology as a space shuttle pilot.

And yet none of it does any good at moments like this.

I hold her hand, and that is enough. It feels like my mother's hand, my wife's hand, or my daughter's hand. It is a human hand. It feels good to hold her hand. It is such a simple thing. It is the best feeling of anything I have done in the ER for several months. For a moment I forget about the anger. I forget about being tired. I forget about everything in my life that does not matter.

Ann is turning white now, right before my eyes. There is not much blood left in her vascular system. It has leaked out into her belly. I look up at the monitor. Her blood pressure now is fifty over twenty-two. Her heart rate is twenty-eight. The lines widen on the monitor, and I see her heart skipping occasional beats.

She opens her eyes again. She turns her head over to me. She smiles—a big smile, a loving, kind, giving smile. It is a precious gift just to me that I will carry forever.

"Thank you, Philip," she whispers.

And then she dies.

I hold her hand a moment longer. It is still warm, but I know she is gone. I keep holding it even after the monitor line goes flat, just to be sure. I don't want to let go first. After all, a promise is a promise.

I stand up slowly. *"How strange,"* I think to myself. *"How strange that this is what I do for a living."*

The alarm on the monitor chimes out suddenly like church bells tolling on a distant hill. I reach up and shut it off.

The room is quiet. I can hear the noise of the ER outside the room. Other patients. Other people. Other problems. I don't want to leave, not quite yet.

For some reason I think of a conversation I had at a party a few years ago. A man who found out I was an emergency medicine physician asked me, "If I find someone dying, and it is too far to get help, what should I do?"

At the time I think I said something about trying to keep an airway open, stopping bleeding, or maybe CPR.

"But what if it does no good?" he insisted. "What if I know he or she is going to die? What do I do then?"

At the time I had no answer. But now, thanks to my friend, Ann, I do. I guess I will tell you since I cannot tell him.

First, it is OK to be afraid. That is normal. Second, introduce yourself, use your first name. Third, hold the person's hand as he or she departs this life.

That will be enough.

Wyoming Snow

Snowflakes the size of a newborn's hand fall against the sliding glass door. I watch as the flakes paint the bottom half of the glass white. Flake by flake they gather along the window, wiping away the black of the night outside. The snow barrels out of the sky, flashing bright for an instant in the security light's beam, only to disappear an instant later, when they meet the warm glass of the window below.

I sit at the workstation, watching the snow. The ER is empty. We have not had a patient in over six hours. The storm has stopped all motion but its own. My lone nurse has disappeared somewhere upstairs into the little hospital to grab a few hours of sleep. I do not mind. For once this place feels safe from the world outside.

I needed to get away. Away from death. Away from the trauma. Away from the endless waves of suffering people. On a whim, I signed up for this three-month emergency medicine job in the remotest part of Wyoming that I could find.

I'd had enough of emergency medicine for a while. As a young doctor, I ran toward the trauma and their accompanying stories, eager for my seat in the front row of The Show. These days I just want to sit and watch the snow fall against the glass during my shift. I need time to think. To untie the knot of stories in my head. People, dates, deaths—they have all blurred together into a tangled mess.

I try to remember to which story each face belongs. The blind child with the burned face—did he belong to the car accident or the house fire? The woman who drowned on Christmas—was she the one with the tattoo of herself on her chest? Or was that the one who drowned in the pond? Or the one who fell off the pier? There are so many faces in my head I cannot keep them straight.

I am disgusted with myself that I cannot remember. I have to remember. I need to remember. Is it not the duty of the living to remember those who are no longer with us? I take a deep breath. Do not get frustrated. Sort them through.

The sliding glass doors across from me light up with two bright beams that interrupt my reverie. Truck headlights reach into the ER entrance and grab me with their light, catching me at the desk, staring into the night. Someone is out. Before I can move, one headlight flickers, followed by the other, as a person walks in front of them.

A fist pounds against the big sliding glass door, breaking the silence. I sit transfixed in the headlights. The fist pounds again, rattling the glass violently, shaking off some of the snow that has gathered on the glass.

Someone is here.

I squint. The bright fluorescent lights of the ER make it hard to see outside into the night. I grab my stethoscope off the desk, sling it around my neck, and jog over to the door. I press my face against the cold glass, trying to see out into the night. An old man, coat hunched up against the blizzard, bangs a fist against the window right where my face is. I jump back.

"Stop looking at me, and open the goddamned door!" he shouts.

I hit the buzzer next to the door, and it slides open. Several feet of snow spill into the ER, jamming the door open. It is everywhere.

"My wife is in the truck—I think she's having some kind of stroke!"

Before I can speak, he hobbles off into the night, lost immediately in the curtains of snow falling from the sky.

With a shake of my head, I run out into the snow. It is middle-of-the-night Wyoming cold. It hurts my lungs to breathe, and I cover my mouth with my hand like a mask. I run toward the headlights, scrambling through the knee-deep snow. I try to step in the man's boot prints, but the drifts in the parking lot are so deep it makes no difference. With each step, my shoes fill with snow.

The parking lot feels like another world. Snow falls past the headlight beams, the flakes from the blizzard swirling and curving every direction but down. I grow dizzy just trying to stay upright. I have to slow my steps so as not to fall.

I see the old man. He is standing next to the open passenger door of an ancient farm truck, the engine still running. The big diesel grows louder as I approach, the *ktunk-ktunk-ktunk* unmuffled by the falling snow. As I near, the man takes a step back and signals frantically for me to hurry.

I grab the door handle to brace myself, wondering if my wet hand will stick to the metal like a tongue in the cold. I round the door. The world slows as I assess the situation.

In the front seat is an elderly woman slumped forward as if asleep. Her head almost touches the dashboard. She wears a blue and red homemade quilted dress with a long-sleeve white top. A small gold necklace dangles straight down from her neck, twisting back and forth in the dashboard light. I can see it is a cross. Two gold, female angels sit on the horizontal beam of the same cross, their bare feet dangling off like children sitting on a swing, their hands clasped together across the apex. It is strangely mesmerizing with the snow falling all around me.

I jump up onto the sideboard of the truck. Snow falls off the roof and onto my arms. I brush it off, balance against the door frame, and reach in. I place my right index and middle fingers on her carotid artery. My fingers listen for a pulse, for life, for hope. She does not move as I touch the skin of her neck. It is as cold as the snow around me. I count sixty seconds to be sure. My hand drops away from her neck.

I jump down off the sideboard and into the snow. I take a deep breath and turn toward the man. "She's dead, sir. She's dead." I say it twice, as I have learned to do. We stand face-to-face. He just stares at me, his body coiled and tense, his hand next to mine on the door. Snow starts to collect on his bushy eyebrows, coloring them whiter than they already are. Neither of us moves.

I start to say it again—louder this time, in case he did not hear me over the sound of the diesel. "She's…" But before I can finish, he jacks me clean across the jaw with a right hook. I see a shower of stars as my head bounces off the truck's door frame behind me. I regain my footing in time to brace myself for another strike.

It does not come.

"You son of a bitch—take her inside and doctor her, or so help me God, I will kill you right here," the old man half yells, half sobs as he raises two ancient fists.

I blink several times, trying to see straight. My ears ring, and my jaw aches from where he hit me. I turn back around and unbuckle the dead woman. With a grunt, I hoist her up onto my shoulders and run through the snow for the ER. I can't help but notice her head is still arched up in the same position, even with her over my shoulders. She is getting stiff. She is not even *maybe* dead; she is *dead* dead.

I stumble, run, slide, and somehow make it back to the ER without falling while carrying the woman. This time I run away from the headlights and toward the giant red Emergency sign above the sliding glass doors of the ambulance entrance.

The door is still stuck open from the snow that is now melting all over the floor. I stagger through the entrance to the little Trauma Room Two, barely able to continue holding the old woman. I look up briefly, hoping against hope that my nurse is around. No such luck. It is still just me.

With a groan, I flop her body down onto the gurney. Her head hits the guardrail on the other side with a loud sickening *thunk*. She is lying on her side, still curled into the sitting position, too stiff to straighten. I try to start with her airway. I roll her onto her back, but her knees remain bent, sticking up in the air. She flops back onto her side. I try again. And again. I can't hold her on her back. I will have to resuscitate her on her side.

I grab my airway equipment to get started. I know she is dead. But sometimes family members need to see me try to save their loved ones. I am OK with that. It is part of the job. I will try for him, even though I know it will make no difference for her. I glance up to see whether he is watching.

The man is not there. He was behind me a second ago in the parking lot. I stop for a moment, unsure of what to do. What if he fell outside? What if he is lying in the snow somewhere between here and his truck? This woman is dead either way.

I curse out loud to the empty room and run back out into the storm. I am halfway across the parking lot before I finally stop. I look around, unable to believe what I am seeing.

The truck is gone. The man left. I am all alone. In its place remain only tire tracks, already fading away in the blizzard. I stand unmoving, knee deep in the snow, unsure of what to do next.

Finally, the big red Emergency sign flickers with a loud buzz behind me, as if calling me back. I turn back toward the ER, back toward the light, and walk carefully back to the only shelter available to me from the storm.

As I return, the nurse is standing in the door. She saw the car's headlights from upstairs.

"What happened?" she asked.

I tell her.

"What now?" she says, looking at the body.

She follows me into the trauma room. The woman's body is lying on the gurney, still curled on her side.

"Help me," I say.

We straighten out the old woman's body so that she is lying flat on her back. We cover her with a clean white sheet, leaving her face exposed. I gently close her eyes so that she looks like she is sleeping.

I take off her crucifix with the angels on it and set it in the center of her chest. Its gold catches the light and shines on the white sheet.

"I'll give John a call. Do you want me to have him come in right now?" The nurse asks. John is our coroner.

I glance outside; the snow is still falling hard on the empty parking lot.

"Tell him to come in when there's some daylight."

The nurse nods. "Call me if you need me."

"Thanks," I say.

She turns and leaves, heading back upstairs for a little more sleep.

I sit down in the room with the woman. I feel bad abandoning her in this empty place, even if she is dead. No one should be abandoned twice in one night.

"Maybe he loved you so much he couldn't stand to see you die," I say to her. "Sometimes that happens. Sometimes it's just too much for people to bear."

She doesn't answer. I look at the floor for a moment. I don't know what else to say.

I lean my head back against the wall and listen to the buzz of the fluorescent lights. I try not to hope, but I do.

Twenty minutes later I hear it.

A truck has pulled into the parking lot. Its old diesel engine runs for a moment, the *ktunk-ktunk-ktunk* unmuffled by the falling snow.

The engine shuts off. A car door slams followed by another and then another.

I walk to the door, hit the buzzer, and stand in the doorway, looking out into the storm. It is still pitch black and snow circles and spins down from the sky in the security lights. For a moment I see nothing.

Then the old man appears. He walks slowly, carefully in the deep snow. He does not hurry. He knows, I realize. He knows she is gone. His arms are hooked with two teen twins about fifteen years old, granddaughters of the woman inside from the looks of them. The man looks fragile, as if he might collapse at any moment. But I know he won't. Not with the two strong farm girls watching his every step.

I stand in the door and hold it for them. I can tell by the girls' faces that they, too, already know. But I can also tell they will be OK. And so will the man. They all have one another in this moment, just as they should, just as everyone should.

Maybe I will be OK, too, I realize. Maybe I don't need to remember the faces of the dead. Maybe I need to remember the faces of the living.

After all, they are the ones who are still here.

Jeopardy

It's Alex Trebek.

The host of the TV show, *Jeopardy!*

I hear his voice coming from the TV before I step into the room. "He occupied a chair over which the sword 'of him' was suspended by a single thread."

I pull back the curtain to the room.

"Hello, I'm..." I start.

A woman holds up her hand, signaling for me to wait.

"Who was Damocles?" the woman says without looking away from the TV.

I stand in the doorway, holding the curtain to the side, still waiting.

A contestant on the TV answers. "Who was Damocles?

"Correct." I hear Alex on the TV say, repeating the contestant's answer.

The woman in the room turns away from the TV with a big smile on her face. She gives me a wave, inviting me in. She appears to be in her fifties. She has gray hair, a kind face, scuffed but nice shoes, a cheap green ring on her right index finger, a frayed, gray, full-neck wool sweater with little blue threads hanging at the cuffs, painted nails, and tired eyes.

She rubs her mother's back.

A tiny woman sits on the gurney next to her. Her back is arched and kyphotic with age. A few strands of thin, white hair are spun across a balding scalp. Her left eye is a solid milky white. I watch as she wipes a few hairs out of her face, tucking them behind her ear with her index finger. The finger is bent back almost ninety degrees, gnarled by severe rheumatoid arthritis. In fact, all her fingers bend in all directions, the joints swollen and deformed from the disease. For a moment I wonder how she picks up food with fingers that flare out so wildly. She senses me staring. Her one good eye turns toward me briefly before returning to Alex Trebek.

According to her chart, she is ninety-seven years old.

"Mom, the doctor's here now." The daughter gives the elderly woman a little squeeze on the shoulder before folding her hands just so in her lap. Her ringed index finger taps. She straightens her back and clears her throat, ready to talk to me.

Introductions are made.

Her mom has been experiencing chest pain for three days, the daughter tells me. It comes and it goes. One moment she is fine, sitting in her La-Z-Boy chair, watching old *Jeopardy!* reruns, and the next she is clutching her chest, with her favorite pink nightie clinging to her skin from sweat. She sweats so bad it leaves a little pool in the chair, the daughter says. The sweating episodes last maybe ten minutes, usually just until the next commercial break.

The daughter laughs and looks away from me, toward her mother. "I'm going to Disneyland—right, Mom? Wasn't that the Daily Double earlier when you started having the pain again?" The daughter reaches up and gently rubs her mother's back in a small circle between her shoulder blades. The old woman just keeps her one eye fixed on Alex, ignoring both of us.

I step over to the bed. "Does your chest hurt right now?"

The woman ignores me.

"You will have to talk really loud. She can barely hear," the daughter tells me. "And she has..." She taps her own head twice right on the temple with her ringed index finger.

I frown, not understanding.

The daughter stands up and walks over next to me. She cups her hands around her mouth like a child telling a secret, and she leans over, placing them against my head, to whisper in my ear. It makes me uncomfortable. "She has end-stage dementia."

I nod, stepping back a little bit for space. The daughter returns to her seat and folds her hands again. The finger taps.

"Are you in pain right now?" I ask in my loudest doctor voice as I examine her.

"Mom, does it hurt right now?" The daughter asks in a loud monotone voice, mimicking my inflection at the end.

The old lady looks at me, annoyed, and leans to her side in the bed, trying to see the TV behind me.

The daughter looks to me and shrugs as if to say, "See—she's demented."

I examine the patient. She is remarkably clean. Some elderly patients arrive with food on their chins. Others arrive with rips in their clothes, snot on their faces, and breakfast on their shirts. But not this lady. She is spotless.

"She looks in pretty good shape for ninety-seven. Does she live at home with you?"

The daughter smiles. "Yes, I take care of her."

"Well, you have done a nice job."

The daughter beams. "I love my mom."

I smile back. "It shows."

An hour later I return with the blood work. Another episode of *Jeopardy!* is on. I stand in the door, waiting.

"They were the Greek female spirits of death," Alex says.

"Who were Keres?" the daughter says to the TV.

"Who were Keres?" a contestant correctly answers.

Again the daughter beams at me.

This time I do not smile back. I sit down between them on the doctor stool.

"Your mom has had a heart attack. Her blood work shows what is called an elevated troponin. Her chest pain is from damage to her heart."

The daughter blanches. Her finger taps faster.

I give my doctor spiel.

"Now, normally when someone has a heart attack, he or she has a procedure done to go in and find the blockage. Once it is found, the blocked blood vessel is opened with a stent. Sometimes a stent doesn't work, and the patient requires open heart surgery." I pause, letting the words hang in the air, hoping she'll jump in. Her mother is ninety-seven after all. But her daughter doesn't say a thing. So I continue.

"How aggressive of care do you think she would want? Would she want to have the procedure for her heart? Or a surgery, if need be? At her age, any procedure is risky."

The daughter just taps her finger, staring at me without blinking.

So on I go. "The other option for her is that we admit her to the hospital, we make keeping her comfortable our top priority, and we manage her heart attack with medications. No intrusive or painful procedures."

The daughter suddenly frowns at me as if my words have just slapped her across the face. She has just realized what I am actually saying.

"If it's something that would help her, I don't want to keep it from her," she says sternly. She walks over to her mother and sits down on the bed next to her. She puts an arm protectively over her shoulders. "Do everything." She stares at me as if daring me to offer her another choice.

I give up. "I will call the cardiologist." I stand up to leave. "We will do everything we can."

"Do everything," she repeats.

I try to smile but cannot. "Will do. Now, are you her power of attorney?"

The daughter has stopped looking at me and is watching *Jeopardy!* again with her mother. "Yes," she says without turning away from Alex.

"Sorry—one more question the cardiologist will want to know." The daughter stares at the screen, refusing to even look at me. "If, for some reason, her heart stopped, would she want CPR or to go on a ventilator?"

"Yes. Yes. I already told you, yes." Her voice rises. Her right hand rests on the bed rail by her mother, her index finger tapping furiously. The green ring clicks against the shiny steel bed rail. "I want you to take care of her. She took care of me. I want you to do everything you can for her."

"Of course," I say as if nothing could be more reasonable.

"Who was Sisyphus?" Alex says as I step out.

An hour later I am at the desk, filling out forms. The telemetry monitor blinks along on the desk next to me. Nine different lines trace out nine different heartbeats of nine different patients in the ER. Beat by beat by beat, they go, marching along at my side.

I check a box on the form in front of me. Just as I look up, one of the lines on the monitor goes flat before squiggling about like a ribbon in a windstorm. The screen flashes red and starts chiming out an alarm. Not even an instant later, the curtain across from me is yanked back. The daughter stands in the doorway, panic on her face.

"Something is wrong!" she screams.

I run around the desk and toward the room. A nurse stepping out of the med room sees me running and instinctively follows.

The nurse, the daughter, and I enter the room together. In spite of the alarms, the little old woman is lying perfectly still. Her eyes are closed as if she is just taking a nap after having baked two dozen cookies for her grandchildren.

The nurse sees the ancient woman peacefully dead and freezes. She looks at me, confused. She doesn't know. So I tell her.

"She's full code."

The nurse presses her lips together until the color drains from them. A frown forms across her brow. I can tell she wants to say something, but she does not. She has done this long enough to know the deal. She nods and steps toward the patient, ready to begin.

I pause, even though I shouldn't. I know what is coming.

"Mom, I love you," sobs the daughter. I move her gently aside. I grab a step stool and set it next to the bed. I step up and then place a palm just to the left of the patient's sternum, the other hand joining atop the first. I take a deep breath and start CPR while the nurse prepares the defibrillator.

With CPR I have to compress her chest hard enough to squeeze the blood through her heart. So I do. But her heart is hidden behind a brittle ninety-seven-year-old rib cage. I press down. Her ribs crack and snap beneath my hands like frail twigs. Hands that took an oath to mend bones instead breaks them.

I look up for the nurse. She has ripped open the giant sticky defibrillator pads and is ready. I lift my hands, and the nurse slaps the first big white pad just above the patient's left breast. I roll the patient away from me and toward the nurse. She leans forward and slaps the second pad on the patient's left shoulder blade. I lay the woman back flat.

I resume CPR, and the nurse turns around to the defibrillator, flipping switches as if we are in a plane and she is the pilot preparing us for an emergency takeoff.

It has been twenty seconds.

The daughter stands behind me, repeating to herself over and over as if in a trance. "Mom, I love you, I love you, I love you."

People are flooding into the room now, responding to the code call. An ER tech shows up, replacing me on the stool with fresh arms that are ready and eager to administer CPR and save a life. I move to the head of the bed, where I belong.

"Hold compressions," I state. CPR stops. I look to the monitor. Her rhythm is unchanged. She needs electricity.

The whine of the defibrillator charging up fills the room. Nobody moves.

"For forty dollars, who wrote the hit song 'What Is Love'?" Alex Trebek interrupts. The audience on the TV laughs at something I can't see. This time the daughter doesn't answer.

Her mother's heart is in ventricular fibrillation. Inside her chest, it writhes and bucks like a fistful of living earthworms tossed into a campfire.

"Do it," I say, nodding at the nurse.

"I'm clear." She looks at her own hands. "You're clear." She looks at mine. "We're all clear." She looks around the bed one last time to make sure no one is in contact with the patient or the gurney.

She punches the big red button on the defibrillator with the lightning bolt on it. Two hundred joules of electricity tear through the ninety-seven-year-old chest, right through the heart trapped between the pads. The defibrillator makes a sound like a ball dropped into a metal bucket. "Kuh-dunnnnk."

The old woman's chest contracts with the electricity, her shoulders rising off the bed and curling inward slightly. I look at the monitor. Still in V-fib. We shock again. And again. Check for pulse. None. Asystole now—no pulse. A tech restarts CPR.

"Give her an amp of epi and draw up some Amiodarone, I say. I crack open our airway kit, grab my Mac 4 blade, snap it together, and stick it into her mouth.

I squat down at the head of the bed, my face right next to hers, and I look along the blade into her mouth for the vocal cords tucked away deep inside. The little light on the end of the blade shines into her airway. With a twist of my wrist, I see the white V-shaped cords looking back at me. They dance about from the chest compressions above.

The respiratory tech hands me the endotracheal tube. As I slide it in between the vocal cords, I can't help but notice that her one good eye has opened, the pupil large and dry. It stares at me.

I finish intubating her. Her airway is secure.

We check the rhythm again. She is back in V-fib. The alarms chime and ring. Push Amiodarone. Shock again. The nurse yells, "Clear!" I let go of the tube. The defibrillator's whine again fills the room with its rising, ominous sound. She pushes shock. Another two hundred joules tear into the woman. Same rhythm, shock again; same rhythm, shock again.

Each time the sequence is the same. CPR stops. Defibrillator whines. Nurse chants. I'm clear; you're clear; we're all clear. Shock. Arch. Nothing.

The tech resumes CPR. More ribs snap. Next to me at the head of the bed a blue-gloved respiratory tech squeezes a purple Ambu bag, pumping air into the patient's lungs through a clear tube. Vomit mixed with a tiny bit of blood leaks from the corners of the old woman's mouth. A new tech with fresh arms attacks the next round of CPR.

The daughter still stands back, whispering over and over to herself. I notice she is timing her words to coincide with each compression of her mother's chest. "I love you mom,"—push—"I love you mom,"—push—"I love you mom,"—push. The tech pumps away to the rhythm of her words, intentionally or not, I can't tell. The alarms ding in time, and the room fills with a surreal symphony of sound with me as the director.

"Hold CPR," I say, stopping the music. We check the rhythm. Still no pulse. The monitor shows the patient is in a pulseless rhythm called PEA.

"Resume CPR," I say and the show begins again without missing a beat.

We inject epinephrine, atropine, dopamine, fluids, bicarb, and ourselves into the effort.

The woman's chest is now like a pillow, collapsing impossibly inward with each compression of CPR. The rhythm changes. We shock again and again.

I turn to the daughter. "She's not going to live."

"Don't you stop!" The daughter leaps forward and points her finger in my face. "I love her."

I want to ask, *Does this look like love?*

But I don't.

Instead, on we go.

We shock again. And again. The smell of electricity and something else unpleasant fills the air.

We inject more drugs. We shock an impossible number of times.

For fifteen minutes, I use every trick in the book—every single thing I can do—to force her to live a little longer—all the while inside hoping that death has taken her away, away from this violence.

A second daughter arrives with paperwork.

She tears back the curtain to the room and shouts over us all. "She is supposed to be a no code! She never wanted this." She glares at her sister. "Here—here is her signature. The papers prove it. She is DNR!" she yells.

Before anyone can react, the first sister grabs the paperwork from the second and shoves it underneath her frayed gray sweater so that I cannot see it.

I am trapped, and she knows it.

"Who has the power of attorney?" I ask.

"I do," they both say. They turn on each other, driven mad from the horror of the moment. They yell. They argue. They cry.

I look at the old woman. She has been incontinent of stool, and her tiny legs are stained with feces. The smell of urine fills the room. Her endotracheal tube dangles from her mouth like a giant plastic tongue. Her chest is collapsed. Her stomach is distended. Blood is on her arms where the IVs leaked. I can smell the defibrillator.

It is my turn to do CPR again. I switch out with the tech. He drips with sweat. I start again. CPR continues.

But still, the sisters argue.

On and on and on, the code runs. I feel like we are all trapped in some kind of purgatory from which none of us can escape. The sisters shout at each other. I fear they may come to blows.

More CPR.

More snaps under my hands. I feel sick, and suddenly I can't remember how many ribs are in a chest, but it must be a lot.

Finally, fifteen minutes after it all started, it ends.

They agree. They say the magic words together.

"Stop the code."

We stop the code.

The monitor flatlines.

She is dead.

For a moment no one speaks.

Then, the first daughter steps up to her mother's corpse. "I love you, Mom," she says quietly.

The second daughter, not to be outdone, pushes forward, shoving her sister out of the way. "*I* love you, Mom." She gets in the very last word, the very last little bit of love.

I find myself wishing they would just stop and go away. I don't think I can handle any more love in this emergency room for quite a while.

I snap off my rubber gloves, tear off my yellow gown, and throw my face shield into the trash.

I step outside into the ambulance bay for a moment to clear my head and stop my hands from shaking.

Some days I am ashamed of what I have to do to make a living.

Otis

Facts collect and gather on my patients like the crows that collect and gather on the power lines strung above the hospital parking lot. The more facts I collect about a patient, the more likely they will coalesce into a noisy flock and take flight together as a story.

————

I stand at the bedside. White hospital sheets are bunched up at the bottom of the mattress into a little pile, half wrapped around a pair of bony ankles. An old man lies on his side, curled up tightly from contractures that trap his arms and legs into the permanent bends of flexion. An angry bedsore on his hip tells me he has been left somewhere curled up in a bed, unattended for a long, long time.

He is tiny. The ten-year-old boy I saw for strep throat a few patients ago was bigger. The man's body is sharp, angulated, and bony, yet it still coils neatly into a ball. It is wound so tight that I bet he would tear in half before we could straighten him out.

Bent knees press up against his chest, and elbows flex as tightly as they can go. The back of his right hand just touches his mouth, triggering some ancient reflex still at work deep in his brain. I watch as dried lips quiver and suck against the hand by his face, as if the morning nap has finished and it is time to feed. His body lies naked except for an oversized adult diaper stamped on the side with the words "Stanton County Medics." I half expect at any moment two young parents to step into the room and claim him as their newborn son.

The little man pants away in the bed while I stand over him. Clear plastic tubing of the nasal cannula, attached to deliver oxygen, dangles halfway out of his nose, hanging at an angle across his face. With each gasp, the tube swings out and back from his lips, fogging slightly, like some sort of odd metronome set to the rhythm of his breath.

———

I stand there observing him. I can feel the crows begin to gather in my mind. I shake my head, and they scatter away, back into the trees—for now.

———

I work my fingers down around a wrist flexed up against his chin. The tips of my fingers search and probe about until they find his radial pulse. The monitor over the patient's bed shows his heart rate, his blood pressure, and even his oxygen level. Yet those are just numbers on a screen. My fingers ask questions the monitor cannot answer. How does his skin feel? Is it warm or cold? Clammy or dry? Flaky and sick or smooth and healthy?

I count the beat of his heart with my fingertips for thirty seconds and multiply by two. Just like the monitor, I calculate his pulse to be fifty-four beats per minute. But unlike the monitor, my fingers tell me his pulse is weak and tired. It has no snap against the volar pad of my index and middle fingers. There is no tiny hum, buzz, or bound like that of an athlete's pulse. Instead, it is just quiet steps that plod along and bide their time.

"Mr. Helfand," I say. "Sir, can you hear me?"

The lips quiver, the oxygen tubing swings, but the man does not answer.

I give his tiny shoulder a gentle shake.

"*Mr. Helfand.*"

Nothing.

I twist his patient ID band in search of his first name.

"Otis," it reads.

"Otis—hey, Otis," I say.

Nothing.

"You guys OK in here?" The charge nurse stands in the doorway, looking at me. He frowns, but he always frowns. He is the charge nurse, after all. Today is a busy day in the ER. The charge nurse is the director of the show. He is the one who fills the rooms, takes the calls, staffs the nurses, talks to the medics, and finds the family members who have wandered off to the cafeteria just when the doctor needs them the most. He knows all the patients' stories, where they came from, and where they go back to—or which beds upstairs they will be admitted to. He is a master juggler with one too many balls in the air. No wonder he frowns.

"What's the deal with this guy?" I ask. "He can't seem to tell me anything."

The charge looks at the man in the bed for a moment, and the frown on his face grows deeper. "I think that's the stroke guy some adult home sent in. Supposedly he was breathing funny, but I don't know. They said he was on hospice, but someone sent him in anyway." He shrugs. "Doc, the medics are en route with a code—CPR in progress."

Just as he finishes the sentence, both of his portable phones ring at the same time. For a moment, I think he might throw them at the wall. But he does not. Instead, with a violent motion, he punches the green button on the first phone with his thumb and holds it up to his ear. "Charge" is all he says. And just like that, he is gone.

I'd better hurry up if a code is coming. If this little man really is on hospice, there is not much I need to do. You do not get on hospice without a terminal diagnosis.

I look down at him lying in the bed.

I wonder what his life was like in such a tiny body. Did people mock him? Did he laugh about his size and use it to clown about? Or did he rage, picking fights he could never win? Did he marry? Was his partner his size? Did he have any children? If so, were they small too? What stories are locked away forever inside his tiny frame?

————

Each new question is another crow that glides down from the sky to land on the wire with the others. A flock is forming; a story that needs telling begins to take shape. I try to ignore them, to stay on task.

————

On his left wrist are two bright rubber bracelets. One red, one yellow. The red one is stamped with the letters DNR. Do not resuscitate. That means no chest compressions, no electrical shocks to the heart, and no tubes down the throat or ventilators for breathing. The other band, the yellow one, is stamped CCO. Comfort care only. That means do whatever you need to do to make sure he is comfortable and do not do anything to make him uncomfortable. The goal is to minimize suffering at all times as the end nears.

In a strange way, those two little bracelets make my job much easier. Instead of a time-consuming work-up, they mean a quick physical exam to rule out acute trauma or infection, then maybe a minor medication adjustment in an attempt to give him just a little more relief, and finally, an ambulance ride back to the adult home until next time.

I start my physical exam.

The first thing I notice is the asymmetry of the man's shoulders. The middle of his left clavicle has a big step-off, resulting in one arm hanging slightly lower than the other. Even curled in a ball I can see it. It makes him look like he is leaning to one side, falling over in place. Maybe he fell out of bed at the adult home and no one reported it. It would not be the first time. Maybe that is why he is breathing fast—because he is in pain. Or maybe it is just an old injury and nothing more. The only way to know is to check it for tenderness.

I palpate along the bony structure with my fingers, pushing gently along the left clavicle while watching his face for any sign of pain. My mind starts to run through the possibilities of what could have happened to his collarbone.

And just like that, before I can stop them, the crows spread their wings together and lift from the wire. A story, a flock, a collection of crows, takes flight as one for the blue sky overhead.

———

She froze.

She felt the call before she heard it.

Then it came.

"Mom!"

She stood at the counter, listening for the tone of the second cry.

"Mommy!"

She dropped the dough and ran.

The boy screamed again, his voice growing louder as he sprinted toward the house. Two little arms pumped furiously in time with his feet as he ran all out for the farmhouse just up the rise. "Mommy!" he yelled again as he leaped over the beat-up bicycle left on its side in the dirt driveway.

"Otis is trapped!"

A red door burst open on the front of the farmhouse. The woman appeared. She stood in the doorway with hands covered in bits of dough. A blue apron hung about her neck. Patches of bright flour painted the front of her apron like fresh white lilies against a summer sky. She stood for a moment, waiting for the boy as he ran toward her. With the back of her arm, she wiped the August sweat from her forehead.

"Otis is trapped!" the boy sobbed. "He climbed up on the roof of the old barn and fell through." The boy was hysterical. "I told him not to go up there. I told him."

The woman squatted, hooking the doorknob with her elbow, and pulled it shut behind her. "Dammit, Danny, I told you to watch him!"

She held up her hand, blocking the afternoon sun from her eyes. Little bits of flour sprinkled down past her field of view. The roof of the old barn was just visible out in the south field. It stood, sun bleached and fading, surrounded by tall wheat awaiting the fall harvest.

She gasped and covered her mouth when she saw it. A hole the size of a small boy had been punched in the center of the half-collapsed roof. Fear tightened her chest and squeezed the air from her lungs.

Otis.

She grabbed the sides of her dress with her dough-covered hands, lifted the bottom of the fabric just above her ankles so as not to trip, and leaped forth off the porch toward her youngest son.

She ran through the tall wheat. A breeze ran through the field with her, sending the heavy brown heads of the wheat rolling about her like waves on the sea. Grains clung to her dress only to be brushed away as new stalks swept the fabric. Danny ran behind, following the trail of the folded wheat across the field.

"Otis!" she cried out as she neared the barn.

She knew this would happen. How many times had she asked her husband, David, to tear down the old barn? How many times had she said that the boys would end up playing on and in it until one of them got hurt? They had just built a brand new barn; there was no reason to keep the old structure standing, especially with two young boys running about.

After weeks of arguing, David had finally conceded. He would tear it down for scrap. Then, one moonless night two months ago, the neighboring farm had its brand new John Deere tractor stolen right out of the fields. David was beside himself. They were already up to their eyes in debt. If they lost a tractor, they would be bankrupt and lose the whole farm. So instead, like every other farmer in the valley, he bought a lock and kept their extra farm equipment safely tucked away in the old barn.

She reached the door with the lock and instinctively yanked against the big metal handle. The door rattled and squeaked but didn't open. A muffled cry drifted out of the barn. Fear surged through her, driving her to a panic over her injured son.

"Otis!" she screamed.

No answer came. She threw herself against the door over and over, trying to break it open. But the big door would not budge. Danny kicked and screamed against the door with her, terrified by his mother's fear.

She ran around to the back side of the barn. Wooden shipping crates rested on the ground, scattered about. Several of them stood stacked against the barn's side where the boys had used them to climb up to the old ladder hanging down from the roof. It took her a moment to realize there was no way in.

She ran on, around to the next side of the barn. She stopped. A small window stood boarded up just a few feet off the ground. Resting against the boards of the barn was an old, rusted irrigation pipe. It had been recut, set down, and forgotten about.

"Mommy, I'm hurt." The cry came again.

She grabbed the pipe and swung it violently against the boarded-up window. It struck the wood with a loud crash, sending splinters into the air. Over and over she smashed the boards that held her back from her son. Inside she could hear Otis crying.

"I'm coming, Otis! I'm coming. Just a minute more."

When the pieces of wood blocking the window were nothing but shards of pine, she dropped the pipe in the dust. She grabbed the spikes of wood in the window frame blocking her way and tore at them like a wild animal. Her hands bled, leaving red marks on the windowsill and wood. But still she did not stop. If Otis had landed wrong or on a piece of sharp farm equipment…She shuddered and tore harder at the wood.

When it was cleared enough, she climbed up onto the windowsill and fell through the window frame onto the dirt floor, landing with a crash on her side. She stood up.

A beam of light shone down from the hole in the roof. Dust from the barn glittered in the sunbeam. At the bottom of the beam of light sat a boy. He was six years old. He sat on a bale of hay where he had landed, his legs too short to touch the ground.

She ran to him and knelt next to him in the dirt.

"Otis!" she cried, taking him in her arms. "Otis." After a moment, she pushed him back to look at him.

His face was filthy. Dirt, tears, and sweat were smeared about. A large red gash ran down the left side of his nose, just missing his eye.

As he sat, he cupped his left elbow in the palm of his right hand, trying to support the shoulder as best he could. His left shoulder sagged, giving him the appearance of leaning to the left, even though he sat perfectly upright. His shirt had been ripped off, and it dangled from the roof above, flapping in the breeze like a miniature flag.

"I'm sorry, Mama!" he cried quietly.

"Did you hit your head?" she asked.

Otis nodded.

She took his head in her hands, feeling around for any lumps or cuts. Flour, blood, and dirt mixed with Otis's thick hair. He was a mess, but she could feel his skull still solid and smooth. His little head was OK.

With that out of the way, she proceeded to check his shoulder. Starting at the sternum, she walked her fingers along the left collarbone. Otis cried out in pain when she was halfway to the shoulder. It was broken.

She rose and turned to yell to Danny, who was still outside, peeking in through the window frame. Her eyes adjusted to the low light inside of the barn. And then she saw it. For a moment, she stood, unbelieving, forgetting about her injured son.

There, in the darkness of the locked barn, stood the neighbor's stolen, partially disassembled, brand new John Deere tractor.

———

"Doc."

"*Doc!*"

I shake my head as Otis, tractors, barns, and crows scatter. I stop pushing on the collarbone.

The charge is back, standing in the door. He is wearing a bright yellow trauma gown and is holding one out for me.

"We need you in Trauma Room Two, Doc. The code has arrived. Didn't you hear the page overhead?"

"Sorry," I mumble as my face suddenly feels hot.

He looks at me for a moment and laughs; he has worked by my side long enough to know me.

"No worries—they just got here." He tosses the gown to me, and I catch it.

I will have to finish my exam later.

I follow the charge out the door. Three policemen, two medics, and a man in bicycling gear are arguing in front of Trauma Room Two. A pair of scuffed cycling shoes are just visible on the gurney inside the door.

And just like that, the crows begin to gather once again…

Honor

Whatever, in the course of my practice, I may see or hear
(even when not invited), whatever I may happen to obtain
knowledge of, if it be not proper to repeat it, I will keep
sacred and secret within my own breast.

—FROM THE HIPPOCRATIC OATH

I step into a room full of tears. Four generations of family are crowded into Trauma Room Two. An old man in a cowboy hat, who is obviously the patriarch, sits by the bed. As I enter, he gives a nod, and three generations file out without a word.

The gentleman in the hat who sits by the bed looks to be about ninety. He wears a tan felt Stetson cowboy hat. It is a dress hat. The felt is clean and smooth; there is no dirt or grease smudged across it like a working cowboy hat. A small black leather band is braided around the base with a sterling-silver clasp on the right side. He has dressed up for this visit.

"Good morning. I'm Dr. Green, the emergency room doctor," I say.

He looks at me. His eyes are pale blue. They have a pleasant emptiness, a wide open sky quality about them. They are not unlike the curved dome of blue that stretches from one edge of a vast free range cattle ranch to the other. I watch as they blink and focus. Creases at the corners form, branching out like dynamic tree roots, emphasizing the depth of the eyes from which they grow.

But it is his mustache that draws my attention. It is as wide as his cheeks, a perfect mirror image of handlebar symmetry. Each side tapers down to a fine thread before turning upward to culminate in a sharp point.

"Morning, Doc." He stands up slowly as old bones audibly grind and pop, extending his right hand.

We shake.

The grip is strong. Rancher strong, even at ninety. The hard calluses cut into the soft skin of my hand. Calluses earned from a lifetime of working fence lines, roping steer, and wrestling cattle.

"Amos," he says.

I nod.

He wears a bolo tie. It is a black braided line that matches the leather one on his Stetson. It hangs down below his neck. A sterling silver steer's skull pulls the two lines together at the top of a fine, white long-sleeve cotton shirt. It is pressed and clean. For a moment I pause, thinking, is today Sunday? He looks like he could be headed to church in his Sunday best.

"What happened with Shelly?" I ask.

His face falls.

We both step over to the bed.

What is left of an old woman lies on her back. She is strapped down to a hard orange backboard. A white plastic cervical collar is Velcroed shut across the front of her neck, still in place from when the medics picked her up. The collar keeps her from moving her neck in case the bones are broken deep inside.

The collar is not made for comfort. It is made to hold drunks, traumas, and combative patients perfectly still. On a little old lady, it hardly fits at all. The front of it has slid up just over the bottom half of her chin and onto her mouth. She chews the top of it like a rabbit nibbling on a carrot in a garden.

She moans as we step near.

"She fell, Doc." He shakes his head slowly from side to side and rests both hands on the bed rail. The lines of his face sag. For a moment I glimpse an image of him looking over a fence at a sick calf lying in the dirt.

I stand opposite him. I rest my hands on the bed rail on the other side. He picks up his right hand and starts twisting the point of his mustache, winding it back and forth between the pads of his index finger and thumb. It is an unconscious action. I see now how he keeps the ends of his mustache so finely pointed.

His wife makes a noise.

We both look down at her. Most of her hair is gone, leaving her almost bald. A few long white strands linger in place. They are stained red from the oozing gash across her forehead. We both watch as a single bead of blood drips down her temple leaving a perfectly straight red line behind it.

Amos pulls out a white handkerchief and gently dabs it away. She looks up at him and then at me.

"David," she says.

He ignores her and wipes the blood again.

"She has dementia?" I ask, already knowing the answer. I read her chart before I came in.

He takes in a deep breath and begins.

"Been ten years of hell, Doc," he says quietly.

He dabs the blood again.

He tells me of the first time. The day he came home after branding cattle all day and found her out back, walking through the property and looking for her sister. A sister who had been dead and gone for fifty years.

He tells me how things got worse. How she started forgetting to turn off the stove. Forgetting to turn off the bathwater. Forgetting her phone number, her name, his name, and their kids' names. One by one, the memories disappeared like a herd of cows dying off from rinderpest.

He tells me how she had always said she never wanted to be put in a nursing home. How they had talked when they were young about living to the end together on the ranch at the foot of the mountains. He tells me how they had promised each other, no matter what, that they would never allow the other to end up locked away in town under a roof with the other old people, away from the sky and the cattle and each other.

He tells me how every single night now, when darkness comes, she screams and cries and paces the house. How it goes on hour after hour after hour. How he has to lock her in a room from which he has removed all the furniture except for a mattress on the floor. Even then, he says, she stands at the door and cries. All night she pounds away with her fists, yelling and shouting about the Mexicans who are in the room with her that only she can see.

I move his hand away from the cut and hold a four-by-four-inch white cotton bandage to the bleeder. I press down just enough to make it stop.

I have heard this story too many times from too many old men, too many old women, and even too many daughters and sons. I watch as he talks. His big frame hangs as if he is carrying an oversize calf across his back, bending him forward, pulling him down, and knocking him off balance.

How many times have promises been made by people who have no way of knowing what it is they promise? Oaths are sworn based on the abstract idea that love and discipline can win out over age and disease. Sometimes love and discipline do. But more often than not, the promises end up being ropes, the same ropes that guilt uses to lasso families into bad choices and decades of pain. Dementia is the worst of all—a disease that seems to feed on promises and guilt. When you find dementia, you find a family haunted by the impossible choices before them.

"It's OK, Shelly." He rests a hand on her shoulder.

As if on cue, she cries out. "David! David! David!" She reaches up with her broken arm and tries to swing it at the air. She yells in pain from each swing of her arm, but she keeps doing it, her brain unable to make the connection between the motion and the pain.

"David, David, David!" Her brain is like a steer with its horns stuck in a fence, shaking over and over, trying to break free.

I glance up at her husband, Amos. He flushes slightly.

"David was a onetime mistake a long time ago," he says.

I force myself to look back down at her, away from him. I try to give him just a little privacy in what must be the most private part of his life.

"David, is that you?" She tries to sit up, but the straps holding her to the backboard keep her in place.

"Damn near every day now, I have to hear his name." He grits his teeth.

But then his face softens.

He reaches out and very gently strokes her head with his big callused hand.

"It's OK, Shelly. It's OK."

She yells and swats his hand. "Where's David? Where's David?"

"David's here; you're OK. David's here." He strokes her head.

Her face relaxes a little bit.

I step forward to examine her.

"Hold still, Shelly." I unbuckle the cervical collar and feel along the back of her neck with a gloved hand while my other hand pins her head down to the board so that she won't twist or move her neck.

"Get your goddamned hand off me, you cur!" she yells, spittle flying from her mouth.

Amos blushes.

"Shelly!" he says sternly. "Shelly! Be respectful to the doctor!" The tips of his mustache quiver with emotion. "Sorry, Doc. She don't mean it."

"It's fine." I say.

"David," she says.

I listen to her lungs. They are clear. Her heartbeat is loud and strong. I push around on her belly.

She yells again, "Get your hands off me!" She suddenly screams a wild animal scream, as if I am coming in through a window of her ranch house at three in the morning.

It is so loud it hurts my ears. I step back.

The curtain to the room pulls open.

"Doc?" The charge nurse pokes her head in.

"It's OK. We're doing fine."

She shrugs and steps away.

Amos's face is a twisted thread of shame, love, anger, sadness, and hopelessness.

"She was a beautiful woman, Doc." He strokes her head again. "The most beautiful woman I have ever known."

"David," she says.

"We raised three kids together—ran a ranch together. At one point we had over two thousand head of cattle."

I nod, giving him the respect that type of life demands.

"We met when we were teenagers. I was a hired hand on her father's ranch." He twists the tip of his mustache, remembering something that must feel like a million years ago.

"Loved her from the first moment I saw her."

"David," she says. She reaches her unbroken arm up toward the ceiling. "David, where are you?"

He takes her hand and gently rests it back across her chest.

"I was in the Pacific for two years, fighting the Japs." He stares hard at me. "This little woman ran the entire ranch as good as any man. She raised our boys to be men I am proud of." He clenches his jaw again and twists the tip of his mustache.

"I tried to do her right. I tried to do her right."

I stand silent, letting him speak.

"Ten years, Doc. Ten years I have watched her fade away. I change her when she shits herself, and she fights me every time. I pick her up when she falls. I sit with her all night as she cries for that goddamned rat, David. I spoon feed her broth and soup while she spits it back at me. I try to make her feel safe; I try to keep her calm. She's the mother of my children, Doc. I took an oath for better or for worse, in sickness or in health."

His voice cracks.

"I am a man who keeps his word, Doc."

He stops twisting his mustache for a moment. A single tear runs down his face. I guess even old cowboys cry when life becomes too much.

"What happened today?" I ask quietly.

He does not speak.

More tears come, rolling down both of his cheeks.

"I failed her. That's what. I failed her."

Sometimes I am not sure what to say to people, so I say nothing at all.

"David, David, are you there?" she says.

The room is silent for a moment. Finally, I speak.

"How did you fail her?" I ask.

Amos pauses and then continues. "A coyote got in the chicken coop. I could hear the racket out by the barn when I was eating breakfast."

He squeezes the bed rail, ignoring the tears as they fall. I am guessing he is a man who hasn't cried in at least eighty-five years.

But he is crying now.

"I grabbed a rifle and ran out to shoot the blasted thing. I thought I had locked the door to her room." He looks at me with desperation. He says it again. "I thought I had locked the door to her room."

"And then what happened?" I ask in a whisper, suddenly afraid for what I sense is on the horizon.

Amos continues. "She finally fell asleep around five thirty this morning." He blows his nose on his handkerchief, the same one he wiped her face with a moment before. It leaves his gray mustache stained red with her blood.

He continues, talking quietly, just to me. "I been up all night sitting with her, trying to help her. Last night was a real bad one."

Shelly suddenly kicks her heels down on the backboard with a loud bang like a child throwing a temper tantrum. She lets out another wild animal scream. She bucks against the straps once again.

I worry she is just going to hurt herself worse.

"Hold still!" I squat down by her ear. "Shelly, hold still!" I yell.

She freezes, unsure of who I am or who she is.

"She got out of the room when I went outside, Doc. She wandered up the stairs to our bedroom. She pulled all the sheets off the bed and all the drawers out as well."

"How many stairs?" I ask.

"A lot, Doc. A lot."

I nod.

"We had been doing fine. We had been doing fine. I know the two of us ain't gonna last too much longer. We were almost there, Doc. We were so close."

He looks up at me.

"But you know what?"

I am afraid to nod or speak.

"Two days ago she pulled a kitchen knife on my great-granddaughter."

His eyes well up with tears, and his mustache trembles again as he remembers.

"My beautiful little great-granddaughter, Sammy Jo. She's ten, Doc. She's ten." He twists his mustache while he stares at me. I know what he is going to say, and he knows I know. But he has reached the point where he no longer cares.

"Shelly thought little Sammy Jo was a burglar. She grabbed a kitchen knife and ran at her own great-granddaughter. A great-granddaughter I know, somewhere inside all that confusion, she loves with all her heart."

He wipes his tears away with the handkerchief, leaving red streaks across the sides of his face.

"If I hadn't been there…" He pauses.

I stand back.

I saw the paperwork. I specifically looked for it when I saw her CT scan results. When I saw the huge intracerebral bleed from the trauma to her head. She has all the required papers. "Do not resuscitate," it said. "No medical care other than comfort measures."

And then he says it.

"I pushed her. I pushed her as hard as I could from the top of the stairs."

He looks down at her.

"I tried to kill her. I tried to do it quick so she wouldn't hurt. Like a sick calf on the ranch. We don't keep them around when they are festering and hurting and ill. That wouldn't be right. That ain't good for them, and that ain't good for us."

I stand silent.

The date on the paperwork is from twenty years ago. She signed it when she had capacity. She signed it so that she would never have to live like this, I tell myself.

"I tried to honor her, Doc. I done everything for her a man can do. Everything and then some. But she pulled a knife on a little girl. On her own flesh and blood. I know she wouldn't want that."

He strokes her nearly bald head with his long fingers.

He bends down and kisses her forehead.

"David," she says. "David."

We both watch as her breathing slows from the worsening bleeding inside her head.

He stands there holding her hand.

I do not know what to do.

So I do nothing.

We both watch quietly as she fades away.

Ten minutes later, her breathing becomes erratic and then finally stops.

The heart rate monitor overhead flatlines.

She is dead.

"It's over now," I say.

Amos takes off his hat, leans forward, and sobs.

"I tried to honor you, Shelly. I tried to honor you," he says.

In my head I think, *"Maybe you did."*

"Maybe you did."

Distractions

It is a burnout day. Our waiting room is full. The coffee machine out front has been filled more times than the one in the cafeteria. Angry family members, tired of waiting, mill about with scowls on their faces. A woman with a screaming baby stands behind a man holding his abdomen in a long line of patients checking in. Through the windows behind them, an ambulance roars into the bay, unloads a patient getting chest compressions from a frantic medic, and tears back out, sirens blaring for the next patient.

Every emergency department in the world has a bell-shaped efficiency curve. At any given moment, a patient can see where on the curve the ER staff are. A few patients check in, and staff will be moving about at a moderate pace. A surge of patients check in, and staff will move at a very fast walk. A multi-trauma occurs, and staff run.

But if the patients keep coming, something else begins to happen. The top of the efficiency curve is reached. At some point even the best battle-tested staff will become completely overwhelmed. When this happens, they are swept up and over the bell-shaped curve by the flow of patients, only to be dropped off the back side and onto the rocks below.

Mistakes become commonplace. There are just too many interruptions, too many lab results, too many phones ringing, and too many family members yelling about what is taking so long. The efficiency of the entire operation slows down until it finally shatters into a million tiny pieces.

Today is such a day.

The hospital, we are told, is completely full. There are no beds to admit our patients. Five patients on ventilators lie in our ER in drug-induced comas, waiting for beds to open up in the ICU upstairs so that they can be admitted. There simply is no more room. And still the patients come.

We are drowning.

I stand at the desk, taking a breather. My head is pounding because of the noise. I cannot drink any more coffee or move any faster. I am fried. This is my sixth twelve-hour shift in a row. Sometimes I am not sure how much longer I can do this job before I just tear apart at the seams from stress.

The triage nurse walks over with an armful of new charts, dropping them with disgust into the rack. Several spill out and fall onto the workstation next to me. I look over in disbelief, but the triage nurse is already gone, trudging back to the front lines of the waiting room.

I sigh and pick up the chart that sits at the top of the pile. Sore throat for one month. ER room eleven. Female. Age thirty-six. I shake my head. Someone has given up six hours of her day for a sore throat that she has had for a month. At least this will be easy—a turn and burn, as we say—so I can make room for the next patient.

I weave my way down the hall, stepping between patients and families. The police march a man by with his hands zip-tied behind his back and a yellow spit bag on his head. He is cursing and screaming. I give them an extra-wide berth. A group of children run past, laughing and playing tag in the midst of everyone. They jump over a homeless man sitting against the wall who is eating one of our sandwiches from the ER fridge. I almost stop to ask if he is even a patient, but I give up and walk on. Someone else can deal with him today.

I step into room eleven, the Ear, Nose, and Throat room. It is the smallest room in the ER, more of a large closet than a room. There is no hospital bed in the ENT room. Instead it has an adjustable chair like the one at the dentist's office. A little controller hangs off its side on a cord and features icons and buttons that control its position.

Ours is an old chair with buttons I can never work. It takes forever, but if you can figure out the buttons, it can slowly recline into a flat surface. The whole chair can also rise up, lifting the patient so that you can sew a child's ear or glue a cut on a small face without having to bend over a gurney. In the drawers of the room lie the equipment needed for nosebleeds, eye lacerations, and marbles stuck in ears.

Right now, a woman in her mid-thirties sits on the chair. She has somehow figured out the controller and reclined it back just slightly. She sits reading a John Grisham novel with her legs crossed. She looks relaxed and bored. I can almost imagine a hair stylist at work behind her.

She has dark blond hair. A wispy red-orange scarf with a single tuck through it offsets the light gray turtleneck sweater she is wearing. A pair of form fitting black slacks disappear into two mid–calf length leather boots. Each boot has a small stylish heel. Gray socks that match her sweater peek up over the boots just enough to make a fashion statement.

She smiles at me and says hello. On her leg sits a photograph of her with a man about her age and three young children at Disneyland. She picks up the photo and carefully places it in the book as a bookmark. She sets the book in her purse and waits for me to speak.

I introduce myself and try to figure out why she would wait six hours for a sore throat in our ER. She looks like the type of person who would have a primary care doctor and would have no problem getting in for an appointment.

On her ring finger is a wedding ring. It is a nice, midsize, upper-middle-class diamond. The band itself looks to be white gold. They say the average man spends one month's salary on a wedding ring. That would make her husband someone like a family doctor, a lawyer, a banker, or a somewhat successful businessman. Not a brain surgeon or a major CEO but someone successful enough to marry a pretty woman and make her feel good with just such a ring.

"So you've got a sore throat…"

She stares at me for a moment and then gives a small laugh.

"Excuse me?" she says.

I look down at the chart in my hand. It says, "Chief complaint: sore throat." I reread the patient ID sticker at the bottom. Thirty-six-year-old female with sore throat. The chart says ENT Room. It takes me a moment before I realize the clipboard it is on says room five. Someone put the wrong chart on the wrong clipboard, one of the many hazards of a busy ER.

"Looks like I picked up the wrong chart," I say pleasantly as I sit down, though inside I am fuming. Little mistakes like this can spell disaster in a busy ER. When I am this toxic from work, every little transgression becomes nearly unbearable. But I keep those thoughts to myself. Patients don't need to hear their doctor complain. "I'll just go ahead and cross 'sore throat' off the complaint list." I draw a line on the chart, shrugging like it's no big deal.

"So," I set down the clipboard and clap my hands onto my knees, "how can I help you today? What brings you in?"

To my surprise, she does not answer. I try to be patient. In the back of my head, I count sixteen other patients I have right now. As I sit here, waiting for her to answer, blood tests are coming back, x-rays are being done, and CT scans are finishing up. I do not have time to sit and chat as if we are having coffee. I need a chief complaint, a quick history, and a disposition.

Somewhere at this very moment out in the ER, one of those patients is likely to be sick—very sick. With so many people filling the ER, it is a matter of statistics. I need to be out there moving among my patients, seeking out the sick ones, looking for smoke before fire erupts.

The patient in front of me smiles again. It strikes me as a strangely blank smile. A woman like her should be at ease with someone like me. She should be chatty and pleasant, asking me if I know so-and-so, trying to find some common connection between us or between her and my wife. But she does not.

I notice that in spite of her fashionable dress, she does not wear any makeup. That, too, is a little odd for someone like her. She is so calm. She—

"I did something bad," she says, interrupting my thoughts.

I scramble to reassess this situation. Is she here because something is actually wrong, or is she here because she wants someone to play games with? I am not in the mood for this—not today. Sometimes people come in because they want attention from someone, and they know that I have to give them some, no matter how busy I am. I squirm in my seat. I do not have time to play the guessing game. Maybe I misjudged her. Maybe she is not so normal.

Her iPhone buzzes on her lap with the receipt of a text message. The screen lights up with a picture of her alongside the man and three children, the five of them standing somewhere with the ocean behind them. I cannot tell. She ignores it, still staring at me.

"And how can I help you with that?" I ask, trying to keep the sharp edge out of my voice, still completely clueless as to what she is talking about.

"You can't," she answers.

She slurs the word "can't" just a tiny bit. It comes out like "cann't." She clears her throat and then straightens her back, wipes her lips, and tries to cover. But it is too late. I heard it.

The phone buzzes on my belt. I ignore it. A different kind of alarm has started to ring inside me.

We stare at each other. I cannot place what it is about her face that is off. My phone rings again. I still ignore it. I have only a minute more with this odd woman before a critical lab value or a family member or a staff member needs my attention.

She stares back at me with her blank expression. And then slowly I see it—or, more specifically, I do not see it. Her face is too blank. There is no expression. She stares back at me, and I realize there is nobody home. And her pupils—her pupils are just a tiny bit too big for her being in a room with bright white lights. Her face is blank, and her pupils are too big. She is on something.

I decide to gamble. To try to force a tell. I gently probe with just the wrong question.

"Are your husband and children here with you?"

At my words, the blank face erupts with emotion. The eyes glisten with tears, her body slouches forward in the chair, her skin flushes a deep red, and she sobs violently.

Bingo.

"They are gone, gone." She suddenly claws at her face with her fingernails, leaving behind red lines as she sobs. It is an overly violent gesture, one of either severe grief or mental illness. I am not yet sure which. Whatever it is, it disturbs me.

In my head, I run through the list of deaths over the last two weeks. I have not heard about a dead family where the mother survived. I scan back further in my mind. The last one was almost three months ago when a semi crossed the midline and hit a minivan. I shudder. I do not want to remember that right now. But the woman in that one died. I know—I just saw her again last night in a nightmare.

Somehow I always end up hearing about who dies in the ER, regardless of whether I am working or not. Whether it's in the paper, from a colleague, or from someone who knew someone who knew the person who died, word always reaches me. I have found that other ER docs and nurses are tuned to this same frequency that, once dialed in, can never be tuned back out.

"I did something bad."

She starts to cry and will not look at me. I am somewhat confused, but I am also starting to gain a sense of where this is going. I need to push this along as fast as I respectfully can before the next trauma or code pulls up.

"What did you do?" I ask.

She hides her face in her hands as if somehow I will not be able to see her.

We sit for sixty straight seconds. I have so many feelings twisting up inside me. I do not want to be here with this woman. My head and stomach hurt. I am getting palpitations from too much coffee. I have not slept well in weeks. Burnout has torched every area of my personal life. I just need this woman to tell me what she needs so I can move on. Yet I have to wait, to play the game just right.

A full minute feels like a lost hour to me on a day like this. My phone and my pager now buzz together. They are looking for me out there. It is only a matter of time before they find me. But I need to know one thing before I can leave this woman alone in the ENT room.

"I ruined everything we built together. Everything."

Whatever calm, drug-induced demeanor she had is now completely gone.

Her voice cracks as she speaks. "He said I will never see him or the kids again, as long as I live."

So much of my job is pushing and pulling people along when they give me their histories. It is a delicate and complex skill, one that I am still learning even after all these years. One slight tug too much or push too hard, and she will disappear, taking her critical history with her.

"Why would your husband say that?" I ask, almost in a whisper. I can hear the police yelling in the hall outside. I try to ignore them, resting my elbows on my knees, trying to give her the sense that she is the only patient in the world.

She turns toward me and says the words slowly. "Because I fucked our neighbor."

It is sad, in a tragicomedy kind of way, how many times I have heard this story as an ER doctor. Like the same movie that will not stop replaying over and over with new actors, this one also restarts with another patient, another family member, or another neighbor. Regardless, the story is not my problem. But somehow, the end results always are.

"What did you overdose on?" I ask, completely ignoring her statement.

I throw it out there, right into the room before us. I have to catch her off guard.

She covers her eyes with the palms of her hands, pushing hard against her face. Her right arm shakes from the effort.

"I, I didn't mean for anything to happen." She looks up at me with pupils that are getting bigger. She is crying, but her tears have dried up. She talks, but not at me. "I don't even know him. I don't even know him."

I realize she is not going to tell me anything without my having to listen to her story. She wants an exchange of information.

"Tell me what happened," I say.

It spills out of her into the room through slurred words, sad eyes, and a broken heart. Her husband was out of town for two weeks on business. Two weeks. She had the kids, all three of them—every day, all day, all night, all the time. Her parents took the kids one night so she could have a break.

"What did you take?" I ask again. I reach over and push the call button. I need a nurse. This woman needs an IV, fluids, EKG, and a room with a monitor in it, not the ENT room. No one answers. I mash the button with my thumb, holding the remote behind my back.

She does not care. She is slurring her words now. She is not even trying to hide it. She is unloading her story on me, dumping it out.

"I was having wine on the porch when Gary stopped by to drop off some paperwork for Tom. I had only met him once before that. We had a glass of wine and talked. And then we had another. And another."

She sobs and her head starts to sway just a tiny bit.

"What did you take? Was it an antidepressant? Did you take anything with it? I can help you. I can help you."

But I can tell she does not want my help. She wants to die.

"And then we had sex—or we tried to. We were so drunk nothing worked right. It was awkward and awful. I'm awful."

I stand up and lean out the door. Across from me, a nurse is helping an elderly patient into a wheelchair.

"Hey! I got a code white in here! Clear out Trauma Room Two," I say.

The nurse shakes her head and yells across to me. "We got a patient on a ventilator in there right now."

"Well, we are about to have another. Open the room, now!" I yell. The nurse throws her hands up into the air in frustration but runs into Trauma Room Two.

I turn back around. The story floods out of her now that the dam has broken. Her eyes jerk erratically from nystagmus while she speaks. I get the sense it is going to happen any second.

I punch the button on the ENT bed controller, trying to lay it flat. I rip open the drawers, looking for oxygen tubing and IV equipment. A packet with the powder for stopping nosebleeds has ripped open in the drawer and covered everything with a red, sandy texture. There are forceps, packing for noses, fluorescein strips for eyes—everything except the oxygen tubing or IV equipment that I want. I swear out loud. I fling open the cupboards, tearing out towels, blankets, and basins.

"I told Tom. I told him right away when he got back. I have no idea why I did what I did. I love my husband. I never for a second have been unfaithful in the ten years we have been married. Never. Never until that one moment. I love my husband…and he loved me."

I spot it. An unused set of oxygen tubing has been left in a basket full of towels on the counter. I pull it apart and string it onto her nose. Now all that is left is an IV.

"It is going to be OK. It is going to be OK. Just tell me what you took."

I think I know already.

"Just tell me if it was a medicine for depression."

She nods. Now there is only the question of which one.

The dry mouth, the big pupils, the sudden onset, the red skin… it has to be.

The ENT chair is bolted to the floor. I cannot roll her to Trauma Two. She is swaying like a tree in a windstorm. I do not think she would make it if we walked. I look out the door. The nurse is now wheeling into the hall a gurney carrying a ventilated patient. She yells at another nurse and jabs her finger in my direction.

I spot the IV start kit sitting on the counter outside the room. I run and grab it, returning to the room to find her still talking.

"Tom said he would never forgive me. He said I had killed him. That I killed us. He took the kids. He took our beautiful children. He said I will never see them again. I called my parents. They had already talked to Tom. They hung up on me. My own parents hung up on me. Everyone has hung up on me. And I deserve it. I deserve it. I deserve it."

She stops suddenly and looks at me with her huge pupils, forcing them into focus. "I deserve to die and I am going to die," she says, and all of a sudden, I realize this is not a cry for help.

This is good-bye.

She looks at me as her eyes widen and I can tell she is hallucinating. Fear fills her face. Whatever she sees is not pleasant.

I grab her arm and tie the big blue band around her bicep to start the IV. She yanks her arm away, fighting me.

Her words slur so badly I can hardly understand her. "Tell him I am sorry. I am sorry. If I could redo one moment in my entire life, it would be that moment. Tell him I love him and I am sorry."

And then it happens.

Her head extends back as if she is looking to the sky, her back arches, her muscles contract, and a grand mal seizure sinks its teeth into her, shaking her back and forth with its mad fury. She seizes.

I punch the code button on the wall with my fist.

It occurs to me that I do not even know her name.

The code call goes out overhead.

And they come running. My staff. They come running to help. It does not matter that they all are tired and beaten down, destroyed, and far behind because of the sheer volume of humanity pressing down on us. When the call rings out for help, they come running. Goddamn, I love my nurses and staff.

"Overdose, tricyclic antidepressants, unknown amount, unknown time of ingestion!" I shout.

They go to work.

The woman on the bed writhes about, her brain short-circuiting and frying before us. My nurses attack her flailing arms with large-bore IVs while the techs go to work with the trauma shears they carry on their belts. The techs dissect, cut, and carve apart the scarf, sweater, pants, and boots, like surgeons gone mad with scalpels.

Froth and vomit fill her mouth. I hit the wall suction, turning it on and pick up the wand. It makes a jarring sucking sound while I try to clear her airway. I have to move it about to keep it from being trapped by teeth that bang and smack together.

"Got it!" yells one of the nurses starting the IV.

"Give her two milligrams Ativan and an amp of bicarb," I answer. It is injected before the IV is even secured. Somehow someone arrives with a gurney. We heave her writhing half naked body onto it, throw a sheet over her, and run her through the hall to the trauma room while she seizes. Patients and families stand back, gaping at the woman flailing about on the gurney and the staff yelling and clearing them out of the way, as the chaos and madness ooze out of the walls of this place and into everyone.

We get to Trauma Room Two. We wheel her in. The battle starts.

She is determined to die.

I am determined she will not.

Round and round and round we go.

She will not quit trying to die.

But we will not quit trying to save her.

And yet the patients still come, piling up in the waiting room, overflowing into the halls and the parking lot. I can see them outside the trauma room. Waiting for me to finish so that I can sit down with them.

But there is only one right now who I am focused on.

After two brutal hours, my staff and I win the fight.
She lives.
Not by much, but by enough.

———

It is the end of my shift. I am exhausted from the day—beaten down,
worn out, destroyed, pummeled, hammered, smashed, obliterated.

And still the patients come.

But my shift is over. I step into Trauma Room Two to check on
her and finish some charting. She, too, now lies in a drug-induced
coma, waiting for a bed upstairs in the ICU to open up.

The room is empty except for the two of us. The lights are low.
The sound of the ventilator breathing in and out fills the small space.
Her heart beats quietly along on the monitor overhead, the red line
skipping a beat every so often. White sedation and clear saline drip
through tubes that hang over her head, run down into the IVs still
in her arms, and disappear into her blood.

I stare at her for a second, shaking my head. Her name is
Courtney. Courtney.

There is something on the floor by the bed. I walk over.

During the code, her purse was tossed into the little basket under
the gurney. The novel she was reading lies open, and the photo she
used as a bookmark sits on the floor. I pick it up. It was stepped on
during the code. It is dirty, the sides of it twisted up and folded over.
Lines from shoe prints cover it.

I look at the picture. It is her with her husband and three kids.
They are happy and tan and smiling. There is a glow about them
in the picture, the glow families get when they are in tune, in sync,
together.

The ventilator beeps for a second. I look up. The beeping stops.
It is fine. I gently set the photo back in the purse, first wiping the
dirt off onto my scrubs and trying to undo the creases.

I look at her for a moment: the tube coming out of her mouth, her blond hair damp with sweat from seizures, and her skin sickly pale. *"What is going to happen to her?"* I wonder.

I grab the stool and am wheeling it over to the computer when I freeze. The man from the photograph is standing in the doorway, looking in at his wife.

His face looks impossibly old. His shoulders sag, his eyes are red, and his hands tremble.

Neither of us moves.

He stares at his wife.

"Will she live?" he whispers.

"Yes," I answer quietly.

I stand unmoving, fearful of what the next twenty seconds will hold for both of them.

I notice he does not wear a wedding band.

The ventilator breathes. The fluids drip. The monitor blinks. Everything in this room is counting down to his decision.

He does not move. He does not approach her. I watch as his face hardens—just a little, but then a little more. It ages and grows cold right in front of me. The eyes turn to stone.

He has decided.

He hangs his head and turns back to the door—turns away from her.

I feel sick.

He bites his fist.

He walks out.

I try to not look at her. I, too, turn away. I do not want to think about what I have just witnessed. I sit down at the computer. I click through menus on the screen. I double-check my charting. I just want to get it done; I just want to get out of here.

Menu after menu after menu I click through. I think back over today. I cannot do this for a living any longer. I do not want to be trapped in these stories anymore.

Tomorrow I will give my notice. I will quit. I mean it. I will walk away, just like he did. I will leave and forget about today and never think about it again for as long as I live. I swear to God.

The ventilator beeps, pauses, and resumes again. It ticks along, suddenly a pointless sound. The minutes pass.

My charting is finished. I stand to leave.

A pair of eyes peek around the door into Trauma Room Two.

I recognize the little girl from the picture. She has blond hair just like her mother.

"Abby!" I hear a voice.

The man is there. He picks her up. The little girl is crying. She sees her mother and the machines. It frightens her. She hides her face in her father's neck, too afraid to look.

A grandfather arrives and takes the little girl, leaving the man with his back to the room. He stands in the doorway, facing away.

I wait for him to leave again. But this time he does not.

He just stands there, staring out into the chaos of the ER, the chaos of life.

He clenches and unclenches his fists. I count ten times.

He takes a deep breath as if about to dive headfirst into a storm at sea, and then he turns around.

His face is fierce.

I can see it now. He is a fighter. He was knocked down earlier, but he has risen back to his feet. Risen to fight. He will not run again.

He walks slowly over to his wife, never taking his eyes off her.

He sits down on the stool next to her and takes her hand in his.

He weeps.

"Till death do us part," I think.

Tomorrow is a new day for us all.

Please Choose One

Please choose one:
The three words blink in front of me on the computer screen.

Please choose one:

Patient is
☐ *Male* ☐ *Female*

I click *"Female."*

I watch as the auto-template feature fills in the paragraph for me based on my choices.

Patient #879302045
Patient is: <u>thirty-eight-year-old female</u> Status: post<u>motor vehicle accident</u>. Please acknowledge you have reviewed her <u>allergies</u>, <u>medications</u>, and <u>past medical history</u>.
I click *"Yes."*
Have you counseled her about smoking cessation?
I click *"No."*
A little animated icon of a doctor pops up on the screen. His mouth begins to move as if speaking. A speech bubble from a comic strip appears next to it.
"Tip of the day: counseling for smoking cessation is important for the patient's health and part of a complete billing record."

The animated doctor smiles and swings his stethoscope like a pocket watch.

I click *"Acknowledge."*

A new screen appears.

Please choose one:
The patient's current emotional state is best described as:

☐ *Distraught* ☐ *Calm* ☐ *Agitated*

I turn away from the computer to look at the patient. She lies curled in a ball on her side. Her bare feet stick out from the sheets and are halfway off the gurney. I notice she wears a turquoise-blue toe ring. She stares straight ahead. She plays with her patient ID band, twisting it round and round with her other hand. Makeup is smeared around small brown eyes. She stares blankly at the wall behind me. I clear my throat. She doesn't blink. I clear it louder. Still nothing.

I look back to the computer. The same screen is still there.

Please choose one:
The patient's current emotional state is best described as:

☐ *Distraught* ☐ *Calm* ☐ *Agitated*

I turn back around.

Blond hair is matted to the right side of her face where tears have dried it to her skin. A thick strand of it hangs across her eyes, and I wonder if it annoys her. I watch as tears re-form in her eyes and run sideways across her face. A teardrop starts to grow on the side of her cheek. More tears start pooling until finally they fall from her face onto her tear-soaked pillow.

Her chest rises and falls at a rapid pace. She is breathing fast, almost panting. It is a raspy sound. I bet if she spoke right now, her voice would sound raw, the kind of scratchy raw that comes after too much screaming. But she doesn't speak. She just lies there breathing with a thousand-yard stare fixed to her face.

The computer dings.

Please choose one:
I click *"Distraught."*

The computer takes me to a new screen.

Please choose one:
Patient's primary reason for being distraught:

☐ *Emotional* ☐ *Physical* ☐ *Other*

The patient starts moaning. I look over. She makes a guttural sound—just loud enough for me to hear—that is part wail and part cry.

I click *"Emotional."*

That selection triggers a new screen with new choices.

Please choose one:
What is the reason for patient's emotional problem?

☐ *Intoxication* ☐ *Psychiatric* ☐ *Neurologic*

Hmm. I look at her and try to decide which to choose. She is in a hospital gown. Her clothes were cut off with the trauma shears when she came in. She still smells like gasoline, blood, and burnt plastic smoke. It burns my nose sitting this close to her, and it makes my eyes water.

There is dried blood mixed with car oil and dirt on her chest. There is a lot of it. It covers her shoulders and the top of her breasts like a red patchy shawl, yet she is not injured. She has been examined and x-rayed and CAT scanned from head to toe. Her body is fine.

The computer dings again impatiently, prompting me to choose one.

Please choose one:
What is the reason for patient's emotional problem?

☐ *Intoxication* ☐ *Psychiatric* ☐ *Neurologic*

I click the "Next" arrow at the bottom of the screen to try to advance the page without choosing one.

Page incomplete; you must choose one.

My mouse circles the screen hesitantly. I guess I will click… "*Psychiatric*." In a way, emotions are psychiatric, I tell myself.

My choosing "*Psychiatric*" has opened a new screen.

The patient shifts on the bed. I look over. A glimmer on her head, reflecting the fluorescent lights above, attracts my attention. I lean in closer. There are shards of broken up windshield glass scattered throughout her hair. Some are brown from dirt—from where she lay on the ground—some are stuck to her head from blood, and some are scattered on the sheet below her. The shards twinkle on the bed like little stars.

I frown. The nurse was supposed to clean her up. I wheel backward on the doctor stool across Trauma Room Two to the door. I lean my head out through the curtain.

I look around. I spot the patient's nurse. She is sitting on the other side of the ER, working at a computer. I know she is trying to enter data from the patient's visit to get her charting done. "*Well,*" I think, "*maybe someone else can help us.*"

I scan the ER. There are doctors and nurses everywhere down here, yet all those I see sit at computers with their eyes chained to the screens and scowls on their faces while they click and type, click and type. I bet the hospital could burn down around them, and they wouldn't notice.

"Hey!" I yell.

No one even looks up. The clicking and typing continue.

An old man standing in the doorway of another patient room makes eye contact with me. He scowls as he surveys our ER. He shakes his head in disgust. I blush and duck back into the room behind the curtain.

The computer dings twice now, prompting me to hurry up. I remember that my patient throughput time is monitored, reported, and compared to the national average. A timer has appeared at the bottom of the screen, letting me know that I am four minutes and twenty-eight seconds behind the average ER doctor throughput time.

The numbers keep climbing. If I spend too much time on one patient, I will get a letter from administration for not meeting my throughput quota. I wheel back up to the computer.

Please choose one:
Because you chose Psychiatric, patient was offered:

☐ *Counseling* ☐ *Medications* ☐ *Inpatient Care*

A sob racks my patient's body, interrupting me again. She shifts in the bed, leaving crumbling clumps of brown dirt on white sheets. She is absolutely filthy. I wonder how long she lay in that field before someone found her. She still stares at the wall, unresponsive.

I look back at the computer. I didn't offer her any of these things. Maybe I should lie and click counseling so that I can finish her chart.

I click "*Next.*"

Page incomplete; you must choose one.

Please choose one:
Because you chose Psychiatric, patient was offered:

☐ *Counseling* ☐ *Medications* ☐ *Inpatient Care*

I try Alt+Tab. No luck.
> *Page incomplete; you must choose one.*
I give up and click "*Counseling.*"
Another screen.

Please choose one:
Patient responded to counseling with:

☐ *Excellent Improvement* ☐ *Some Improvement* ☐ *No Improvement*

I click "*No Improvement.*"

The little doctor figure reappears on the screen. He's holding up his index finger, and a light bulb appears over his head as if he's just had a fantastic idea that he can't wait to share with me.

"*Dr. Tom Tip reminds you: Did you try offering a drink of water or a tissue? Surveys show that sometimes it's the little things that make patients feel better.*"

I look over at her. I can't bring myself to offer her water. Her knuckles are blanched white from the death grip she has on the side rail. She's mouthing the word "no" over and over to herself and shaking her head back and forth. Her eyes are wide with terror and do not see me. The skin of her face is pulled taut with fear.

I know that look. She is seeing the moment. I know she is going to see it again and again for the rest of her life. It will come in nightmares, it will come in dreams, and it will come at the worst possible moment of what should be happy occasions. More likely than not, it will even come at the moment just before her own death, no matter how long she lives. She will never escape it. Sixty-eight minutes ago, her brain burned an image into the inside of her skull that she will never be able to unsee.

I click "*Skip.*"

The doctor icon disappears and is replaced by text.

Please choose one:
Did you offer the patient water?

☐ *Yes* ☐ *No*

I click "*No.*"

The little figure pops up again—this time with a stern look on his face and his arms crossed.

"*Surveys show patients like it when their doctors offer them water or tissues. Patient satisfaction scores go up. Try it. You might be surprised.*"

He uncrosses his arms and holds out a little glass of water.

For a brief second, I imagine punching my fist through the computer screen. It would feel so good to climb the stairs to the top floor of the hospital with the computer stuck on my arm. I imagine spinning in a circle and launching it as hard as I can off the roof of the hospital toward the pavement below. I would give anything to see it smashed, destroyed, and ruined—to do to it what it has done to the profession I once loved.

But I know they would just replace it with another computer and—just as quickly—with another doctor.

I sigh and look around the room.

There is a cup on the counter.

I frown, as it is very dirty.

I pick it up and turn it over.

A child's tiny bloody shoe falls out onto the counter.

The woman cries out, "Oh God! Oh God! Oh God!" and grabs the child's shoe before I can pick it up.

She holds it next to her face. She's sobbing now and starting to scream. "Oh God, oh God, oh God!" She clenches the shoe to her chest. The blood on the shoe matches the blood on her chest.

The computer dings.

"Did you give the patient a cup of water?"

I lie and click *"Yes."*

"Good job!"

The computer trumpets out a happy horn sound. It's hard to hear over the patient's screaming. The little doctor gives me a thumbs-up and high-fives a hand that appears on the screen next to him.

"Sometimes it's the little things that make people feel better."

I click *"Next."*

The "Patient Disposition Screen" loads.

Please choose one:
Where is the patient going after the ER?

☐ *Home* ☐ *Admitted* ☐ *Transferred*

I hover the mouse on the screen for a second, trying to decide.

I click *"Home."*

Please choose one:
How is the patient doing after your care for her?

☐ *Improved* ☐ *Not Improved* ☐ *Other*

I look at her again.

I click *"Not Improved."*

Warning

This time the whole screen flashes. The little doctor is back, hands on his hips. His face is stern, and the speech bubble appears next to his head. The letters are in red this time.

"*Patients who are <u>not</u> improved should <u>not</u> be sent home. You clicked* <u>Psychiatric</u> *as her primary issue. Perhaps some medications would help the health care consumer. Would you like me to recommend some choices available on the hospital formulary?*"

I ponder the question. Is there a drug for this? Something that will make her feel better? Something that doesn't wear off, like, ever?

I click "*No.*"

Are you sure? The computer asks again.

I click "*Yes.*"

A big red flag now pops up on the screen, and the computer buzzes like a halftime buzzer in a sports game that I have just lost.

A note of this patient encounter has been sent to your hospital administrator for chart review of this patient. It is the goal of our health care facility to make patients feel better before they are discharged. You have acknowledged that you failed to do so. You will likely receive a lower patient satisfaction score for this.

Please acknowledge.

I click "*No.*"

It flashes again.

Please acknowledge.

I click "*No.*"

Please acknowledge.

I click "*No.*"

A box pops up.

I am sorry, valued health care provider—do you not understand the question? Would you like to fill out a service ticket?

☐ *Yes* ☐ *No*

Please choose one.

The words blink at me on the screen.

I look over at the patient. She is on her side again, sobbing as she cradles the tiny shoe to her chest. Her eyes are squeezed shut, and she's rocking back and forth so hard the whole gurney is shaking.

I look back at the computer.

Please choose one.
I look back at my patient.

Please choose one.
Suddenly I get it. I choose.

I reach down and unplug the computer. The screen goes black.

Without the noise of the computer fan whirring, the room is suddenly silent—save for her quiet sobs.

A strange feeling comes over me—one that, after so many years, I almost forgot existed.

I remember who I am and why I am here.

I stand up and take a deep breath. I step toward the patient and begin the long, tedious process of gently picking out the shards of bloody glass stuck throughout her hair. As I start to work, she opens her eyes and blinks.

She sees me.

The terror that fills her eyes fades just a tiny bit.

For once, the computer stays quiet.

I pick through the strands of her hair. The three words blink in my mind over and over.

Please choose one.

Please choose one.

Please choose one.

Ghosts

I once worked in an emergency room with old wooden doors on the rooms. The patterns created by the grains in the wood became Rorschach tests for patients—some saw mountains, some saw animals, and some saw nothing at all. But the door to room nine, directly across from the trauma rooms, was different.

The patterns in that door frightened patients.

It was hardest on the schizophrenics. I lost track of how many times that door crashed open from a panicked kick. Startled, I would look up from my work to see a patient standing in the doorway, eyes wide, skin sweaty, and face pale as if he or she had just seen a ghost. It happened so often that I finally had to make a rule: no more psych patients in room nine, period.

For years I blew it off as a strange quirk until one morning at about three o'clock when I was interviewing a patient. In my sleep-deprived stupor, I sat on the stool next to the room nine bed, the gurney with the patient on it between the door and myself. The door was closed to give us some privacy. I was talking to the patient when the hair on the back of my neck began to rise.

There were faces in the door, watching me.

The grains of the wood wavered between the faces of past patients who had long since died and just a pattern of lines in the door. I sat afraid, frozen in place, unable to understand what they could want from me. Finally, the patient on the gurney before me shifted awkwardly, and asked if I was OK.

That was the first time I ever saw them. I could not understand why they had returned to the ER or what they could possibly want from me. That night was a long time ago, and yet I still to this day am trying to make sense of it.

Sometimes the roughest part of what I do is getting out of bed each day knowing an onslaught of suffering is barreling toward me. Yet, there is nothing I can do about it.

As I wake, drink my coffee, and drive in to work, so, too, do my patients. We all start our day the same way. I can't help but wish there was some way for me to warn them: today is the day we will meet in Trauma Room Two.

At times, I imagine myself as a ghost floating about. I follow behind them, begging them not to glance down at their cell phone on the way to work, pleading with them to stay off Division Street, and imploring them to wait just *one extra second* before they step out into the crosswalk.

Yet, as a ghost, no one can see me, and no one can hear me. My words have no meaning, my warnings no heed, and my panic no justification. Nothing has happened. Not yet. Today is starting out as every other day has started out, and those days ended up fine.

So instead, we all get up and go to work, and the day begins. I arrive at the ER knowing my warnings once again have been lost in the noise of life. All I can do is prepare.

I walk through the department at the start of my shift. Airway equipment—check. Central lines—check. IV equipment—check. Room by room, item by item, I mentally touch and confirm each tool. As I see each item, I make a quick practice run in my mind so that when I need it, I don't have to think or feel. I can become pure action and resuscitation, if need be.

Step-by-step, I approach readiness, while step-by-step somewhere else, another person approaches disaster.

Like two planets whose gravitational fields pull them together, we begin on a collision course, gathering speed and momentum, neither of us yet aware of the other. I know a crash is coming, but I don't know who, what, or where. My day is twelve hours of bracing for impact.

The buzzer on the radio squawks. A car has hit a pedestrian. The victim is unconscious on scene, rigs seven and twelve are responding, and I know our planets are about to collide.

A hush falls over the ER as we listen to the call. The medics are on scene now. It is bad. The victim is a young child. She is critically injured. The car was speeding through a school zone. I suspect the quiet ding of a cell phone text has once again changed the course of the universe.

The medic phone rings, and through the chaos and the static of the call, there is only one thing I hear—the shakiness of the medic's voice. "ETA two minutes," he says. "Extensive facial trauma, chest trauma, maybe a collapsed lung. IV established, patient being bagged, not intubated."

The radio stops. I take a deep breath. My job now is to drain the department of all emotion so that we can prepare. I become a human black hole. We cannot afford to feel. A child is dying. Feeling is for later. Now we must focus. We must move. But we must not feel, or we will lose focus and fail.

My voice is calm and businesslike, as if we are getting a shipment of broken computer parts that require nothing more than reassembly in our shop. Part A will attach to part B, which will attach to part C.

Nothing more.

My voice sounds confident and ready, even to my own ears. It is so convincing that I almost believe it. Yet inside I feel it. The sheer terror. There is no other word. In the back of my head, I can feel the faces of the old room-nine door showing up in force for the show. They stare out at us, watching, observing, and grading. I try to ignore them as I prepare myself to once again, bear witness to a life being torn apart before me.

We scramble to get Trauma Room Two ready. People run. Voices shout back and forth. Tubes are prepared, drugs are drawn up, and machines are wheeled about through the department. One of the nurses hands out bright yellow gowns and blue gloves like bullets and helmets before a battle.

Everyone knows his or her role. The techs prepare the monitors and gurney. The nurses draw up meds one by one, laying the drug-filled syringes out on the counter in a row, getting ready for what-ever comes through the door. Pastoral services arrive with a Bible. I stand off to the side, my head racing through protocols, doses, tube sizes, and backup plans. There is an excited buzz in the air as we prepare. Then it happens.

We achieve readiness.

A silence settles over the room like a lens focusing us into exis-tence. Nothing moves. Each of us feels alive, vivid, and real. Each of us feels anxious, excited, and terrified at what is coming. The colors of the room seem brighter, my friendships with the nurses feel stronger, and my mind feels sharper as I breathe air that suddenly feels cleaner.

I can feel my heart beat in my chest, my hands, my skin—every part of me.

The medics come crashing through the door, CPR in progress, and once again motion returns. As they roll into Trauma Room Two, time slows. I focus all my being onto the little child sprawled on the stretcher before me. She is twisted and broken like a flower that has been stomped down into the soil. I know this battle has been lost before I ever touch my stethoscope to her blood-covered chest.

There are certain things I cannot write about. There are certain things which I will not write about. They are too terrible to share. It is my job sometimes to just keep them to myself. So be it. The next several minutes of that day are holy, private, and terrible. And they shall remain that way forever. Only those of us there that day should be burdened with what we saw. We will carry it for you. We will carry it for everyone.

Suffice it to say, there is now another face that stares out from the door of room nine, watching, waiting, and perhaps remembering.

I know that weeks, months, and years later her face will come to me. I will be camping alone in the desert as far from another human being as I can get. The door of room nine will rise in my mind, and I will sense the faces slowly wandering in from the horizon to take a seat next to me by the flickering campfire.

The desert, the stars, the desolation, and the emptiness are not enough to keep them away.

I will stare into the fire, the smoke twisting like ghosts rising into the night above. I will wonder. Do the stars know? Does God know? Does the dirt know? What is this place, this life, this brief flash of light before we fall back into the darkness from which we arose?

For hours, I will watch the fire dance and the smoke rise. The faces will sit with me. I will feel it. They, too, will wonder about it all. Finally, the fire will burn out, the smoke will stop, and the sun will rise. Two days later I'll have to go back to work. But out there in the desert, I will understand.

The faces will always be with me.

Waiting.

Watching.

Making sure that I will never be alone when the next trauma comes.

Remember This

The end begins with a stomachache.

Lois Drader clips just below the rose, angling her garden shears up slightly to avoid the thorns on the stems below. With a loud snip, the rose snaps free and tumbles to the earth, spinning down through the other red roses of the bush as it falls. She reaches out a hand to catch it, but is a moment too late. It lands between her feet with the other discarded flowers and stems.

Lois leans forward slowly on her gardening stool and picks up the rose with a shaky hand. The flower appears splotchy and dark. She frowns. Damn glaucoma. She moves it around in her field of vision until she finds the spot where she can see it clearly.

She turns the rose over in her hand, rotating it gently, inspecting it for flaws. The smooth red skin of the rose stands in contrast to her wrinkled, spotted hand. "This'll do," she says quietly to herself, nodding. She places the flower into the tin bucket by her feet with the other keepers.

The roses this year are the most beautiful ever. Both of her two rose plants are overflowing with plump, luscious, round roses. The two bushes stand against the wooden planks of her backyard fence. A few red and white petals from each bush are scattered across the ground by her feet.

She glances down into the bucket. Her vision is too poor to see inside the shadow of its edges, but she runs through each rose in her mind. Yes, this year's roses are the best she has grown in the twenty-five years since Henry's death. Tonight would have been their seventieth anniversary. She will celebrate once again with an empty chair across from her, a vase full of handpicked roses as her only companion.

She bends forward on the gardening stool, doubling over slightly. Her stomachache is back. She crosses her arms over her abdomen, pressing against it. Her stomach has been hurting all morning. She counts to ten and the crampy pain fades away.

She sits back up and looks around the bushes in front of her. This time she picks one of the white roses. She slides the stem between her index and ring fingers with her palm up, as if the rose is a glass of fine wine. She pulls it forward, straining the stem on the bush, and smells it. She can just detect its fragrant odor. At ninety-one, her smell is going as quickly as her sight.

She cups it in the palm of her hand, closes her eyes, and runs the pad of her thumb gently across the top of it. The petals are smooth, the delicate edges crisp and healthy. So far the bugs have left this one alone.

She opens her eyes and twists it slightly to the side, out of the shadow of her gardening hat. She moves it into the bright sunlight of the morning.

The pain comes again—worse this time. She forgets about the rose, aware only of the odd sensation in her stomach. She waits. She starts to sweat and her heart begins to race, but just when she thinks she cannot stand it anymore, the pain disappears. Maybe just one more rose, and then she will head inside for some rest.

She looks at the white rose again, absentmindedly sliding her finger back and forth across it. She works her fingers around the side of the flower and down to the stem, trying to decide where to cut with the clippers. It feels stiff. A thorn on the stem lightly pricks her finger, but she does not mind. After decades of gardening, it is a familiar sensation.

She works her fingers down the stem, feeling the grain and the roughness as well as how the stem rises to a point for a thorn. She stops. Her stomach pain is returning. Part of her grows frightened; it is unlike a typical stomachache. Maybe she should go inside and take some baking soda and water. That usually seems to help.

The stem in her hand begins to buzz. It is an odd sensation. She squeezes the whole stem to try to stop it. Her hand wraps around a buzzing bee crawling up the stem, and the bee promptly buries its stinger into the palm of her hand as she squeezes down.

With a quiet gasp, she pulls her hand back. It throbs. She holds curled fingers out into the beam of sunlight before her. She leans in and brings the hand right up to her face. She can just barely make out a tiny stinger stuck in the palm of her hand.

She feels sweaty. The surprise of the sting has caused her heart to race. Now the pain in the stomach comes with a vengeance, pulsating with each beat of her heart. She thinks she'd better get that baking soda; the stinger will have to wait.

She pulls her walker over next to the gardening stool. With a practiced motion, she stands slowly, using it to brace herself. She takes a step toward the house and realizes something is wrong.

Her stomach really hurts now, the pain a deep tearing sensation that pulsates into her lower back and down into her legs. But it is her hand that concerns her. She holds it up in front of her. It looks to be at the end of a long tunnel. She frowns. That should not be. The fingers are drifting farther and farther away from her into the distance. By the time she realizes what is happening, it is too late.

The world goes black.

She wakes up on the ground with a terrible pain, the type of which she has never known, ripping through her abdomen and expanding outward with each beat of her heart. Her head lies on one of the patio bricks where it crashed down, and it, too, pulsates with each awful beat of her heart. Dried blood covers her face from where she has cut her head against the brick. She tries to move, but her arms and legs will not work. She tries to cry out for help, but her mouth just makes sounds that make no sense.

She tries again to yell; this time the sounds are a little louder. The garbled words do not sound like her own. They frighten her. She lies quietly in the grass. The pain in her belly tears through her again, and she gasps. She tries to curl into a ball but is unable to muster the strength. She looks around. She realizes the sun is setting. She is alone in her backyard. She must have been down for several hours.

The pain comes again, lancing through her like a knife stabbed deep into her belly. It is so bad that she feels like she is going to explode out from the center of her body. Her head throbs, but it is nothing compared to the other pain. The sensation comes again, erupting with a fury at the very center of her being. Then something strange happens.

The pain stops hurting. It is still there—she can feel it—but somehow it no longer touches her. It is almost as if part of her has unplugged from the rupturing aneurysm in her belly.

A quiet peace begins to wash over her. She looks at the roses in the setting light of the sun. They are more beautiful than she has ever seen them. She smiles slightly, grateful for the chance to look on them one last time. It dawns on her that she is dying. This is the end.

The world goes black.

A hand shakes her. "Mrs. Drader, Mrs. Drader!" It shakes her again. She tries to say no, but her lips will not work. Her eyes flutter open. A young man comes into focus. He is wearing a medic uniform. The word "Student" hangs just below his name tag in bright orange letters. A second, slightly older man stands behind him in a paramedic uniform. The two of them cast shadows on her rosebushes in the evening light.

"She's waking up," the student says excitedly.

"Check her pulse," the older man says.

She feels fingers on her neck.

"Forty-two," the younger man answers.

The older medic squats down on the other side of her. She feels more knowledgeable hands pushing and squeezing as they check her. When he pushes on her belly, the pain comes again, and she hears herself moan.

"Give me your hand," the older man says. He takes the younger medic's hand and places it on her belly.

"Do you feel that mass pulsating?"

The student nods.

"She has an abdominal aortic aneurism. We better hurry if she is going to have a chance."

She tries to tell them to leave her be. She just wants to watch the last rays of the sun on the red and white roses. But something went wrong when she hit her head on the stone, and she cannot speak.

Lois lies still as they run about. An IV is started in each arm. Fluids are hung. Oxygen is tucked into her nose. They roll her onto her side, and a hard board is placed under her back before they roll her back down. She moves her legs a little bit and realizes with horror that she has lost control of her bladder. It is an awful feeling. She wants to hide her face, but her arms will not move.

She is completely at their mercy.

She half watches as the older medic repeatedly yells at the student. The young man is much too excited for the older man's temper, but they work together, side by side. The medics lift her into the back of the ambulance. It has only been three minutes since they arrived.

The ambulance's engine roars to life. She hears the older medic speaking quickly into the radio as they accelerate away from her home and her rose bushes. The ambulance hits a pothole, jarring her suddenly. The pain explodes through her again, wiping out every other feeling and thought.

She feels herself slide backward, as if sinking down into the depths of a great ocean. Images of her life begin to float past her like slow moving bubbles rising out of the depths and reaching for the surface.

One by one they come. Recent memories first, then older memories, and then the first memories. Each one touches her briefly before drifting on. She wants to reach out and grab them all, but she has no control over what is happening. A memory brighter than the others appears below her. She knows as soon as she sees it that this is the first real memory. It rises up out of the depths in a slow, winding spiral as she sinks deeper and deeper toward it.

And then, like a giant bubble, it encases her.

She is holding a music box in her hand. A white-and-pink porcelain ballerina twists slowly in a circle atop a giant green lily. A small white swan circles in the opposite direction around the edge of the music box. Delicate chimes ring out in the rolling music of Tchaikovsky's *Swan Lake*. Over and over the notes sing as the ballerina twists and the swan swims.

Lois feels the weight of the glass box in her hands. It is heavy and the glass feels cold against her skin. She cradles it between her palms. She remembers this box. It is a going away present from her father. She is five years old. She stares transfixed, watching the ballerina she has not seen in eighty-six years spin before her.

With a shock she notices her hands. Instead of swollen joints with bent fingers, she has tiny fingers. A child's fingers. The music box seems impossibly large compared to them. She wiggles the fingers. They are hers. She feels her father's warm hands on her shoulders as he kneels down in front of her.

He wears an army uniform. A big green bag sits on the floor next to him. He squats, his face inches from hers.

He is crying.

"Remember this moment," he whispers to her. She nods her head slowly. "Remember this moment. Swear it to me, Lois," he begs. Her five-year-old self does not understand what is happening, but she nods her head.

"I promise, Daddy. I promise to remember." He hugs her tightly, the ballerina still twisting in her hand.

He stands. It is the last time she will ever see him. "I must remember this moment," she whispers to herself. "I must remember this moment forever."

And she does.

The colors begin to fade. "No!" she cries. The music box washes away as if it had never been. "No!" she cries again.

"I got a pulse!" the young medic cries excitedly.

Lois feels herself open her eyes. Bags of IV fluids hang above her, waving and shaking about as the ambulance races.

"You are going to be OK, Mrs. Drader," the young medic says. Lois sees blood from her head on his hands.

She feels a blood pressure cuff inflate on her arm.

"Pressure is eighty! Let's go—let's go!" he suddenly shouts.

The whole ambulance shakes as the engine roars, pushing it as fast as it can go. Time is short if they are going to save her.

She feels the pain return. She somehow knows that whatever it is doing inside her is something that cannot be reversed. It feels so final, like the last page of a long novel. Part of her feels sorry for the young medic trying so hard to save her. She tries to speak again, but only garbled sounds come out.

She hears the medic yell, and she feels herself fall back into a great bright space.

She is standing on a hill in eastern Montana. The smell of spring fills the air. A warm breeze gently passes over her. She takes a deep breath and fills her lungs with a potpourri of pine trees, young flowers, and spring soil. She shifts slightly and realizes she is sitting on the hood of a car. The sun is setting. She wears a cheerleading outfit. A makeup mirror is in her hand, held out before her. It is silver and round with a little metal door that clasps closed to protect the glass. But it is open now.

She sees a face in the mirror. It takes her a moment to realize she is looking at herself. How beautiful she is! Her thick brown hair is full and waves slightly in the evening breeze. Her lips are red from the lipstick she holds in her other hand. A few pimples are scattered about her face. A necklace with a single small heart-shaped locket lies just below her chin. She smiles and sees white teeth.

She feels a large arm come down gently across her shoulders and goose bumps scatter down her spine. She knows who it is. She lowers the mirror, barely able to contain herself. In the distance, the setting sun casts longing shadows across the fields and hills. A hawk circles lazily on the rising breeze. Crickets call out in the golden light.

She is with him.

She waits, staring into the distance, almost teasing herself by not looking at him. These are the final seconds before their first kiss. "I must remember this moment," she whispers to herself. "I must remember this moment forever."

And she does.

The red sky tears apart in front of her.

She gags.

The medic is suctioning her mouth with a plastic tube, yelling again. She can feel herself gagging on her secretions. "*No—please no!*" She tries to cry, "*Send me back. Send me back.*"

But the medic suctions her out and holds a bag over her mouth, pushing the air down into her lungs.

She feels a rattle in her chest as the air pushes down through the aspirated fluid. Breathing has never felt so wrong. The sharp pain comes again, and she finds herself trying somehow to will it even more, to tear it the rest of the way, whatever it is tearing inside of her.

Alarms ring out through the ambulance.

"She's going into V-fib!" The young man is panicking.

A voice in the front of the ambulance yells back.

"Well, shock her, dammit! We're almost there. Two minutes. Shock her!"

She hears the rising tone of some sort of machine. It hurts her ears for a moment. She starts to slip back into the fade. This time the world disintegrates around her into a gray, formless void. The pain in her belly stops.

She is back in the sea again with the memories bubbling past. This time it feels familiar, even safe. She watches them float by with delight, breathlessly waiting for one to take hold.

And then one does.

A hand knocks on a wooden door. "Two minutes!" a voice calls out. She hears giggling. She knows those giggles. She turns around and her sisters are there. All three of them. Each hugs her and talks of her beauty. She hears herself speaking with them, joking with them, crying with them, and just being with them. Oh! How it makes her heart ache with love to see them!

The three young women stand back, looking at her. Their faces are glowing, and their hair is done up in curls, folds, and twists that have taken all morning. Their peach bridesmaids' dresses shimmer in the sunlight coming in through the church window.

It is her wedding day. Her youngest sister steps to the side. A full-length mirror shines out. She sees herself. Her wedding dress is new and white. Her skin is tan from the summer sun. She turns in a circle slowly, watching the lines of the dress follow her around in the mirror. She looks at her body in the dress. It is thin, tight, strong, and flexible, and she moves easily, taking joy in her youthful elegance.

A second knock comes at the door. He is here! Her sisters laugh, and she runs to the door. The voice starts to speak on the other side, and she hears herself say, "Come in! Come in, future husband!" Her sisters laugh, and she laughs too. She feels a smile beaming from her face as she reaches for the door handle.

"I must remember this moment," she whispers to herself. "I must remember this moment forever."

And she does.

A flash of white electricity yanks her back.

Her eyes are already open as she returns. They focus. The medic is sweating, the veins on his temples bulging. He holds a white paddle in each trembling hand.

"I got her! I got her back!" he screams.

"*No!*" she cries again, trying to go back, trying to open the door, to see his face. "*Oh—please, God, send me back. Send me back.*"

But it is to no avail.

The ambulance stops. Its back doors swing apart. She feels the medic suction her mouth again. Nurses jump up into the back of the ambulance to assist the medics.

The stretcher is lowered out of the rig and into the ambulance bay. She feels something flutter about inside her. It does not hurt or alarm her. It feels as if a sparrow has been trapped in the center of her chest, and it is beating its wings against her ribs, trying to escape.

"Call the code!"

One of the nurses screams as the monitor sounds off loudly again beside her.

"Call the code!"

Lois lies still as they run the gurney into the emergency room. Doors fly past. Patients fly past. A wide-eyed child standing in the doorway of one of the rooms stares at the dying old woman wheeling past. She tries to smile, but her face will not work.

They wheel her into a room called Trauma Room Two.

A doctor runs toward her, his long white coat flapping behind him. The doctor fades and the coat flaps. Only now it is not a coat; it is a white curtain on either side of a window.

The window is propped open. The roar of breaking surf echoes in the distance. She breathes in and smells the tropical sea and feels the warm night air. Without moving her head, she can see the moon rising over the ocean. Its reflection dances on the waves, painting an off-white path through the blue night toward the horizon.

She wonders where it leads.

She is naked.

She feels his warm skin touching hers. He sleeps beside her. A quiet peace fills every pore, every crease, and every curve of her being, all the way down through her bones and beyond.

She smells him. He is the smell of the sea and the sky and the pine trees. He is the smell of the stars and the waves and the moon. He is the smell of hope and love and peace.

She presses her entire body against his. In his sleep, he presses back, encircling his arm over her. There is no space between their bodies—no space between them.

Time passes. The first rays of the sun break on the distant surf, the roar rolling in through the window. She kisses his arm, tasting the salt of his skin on her lips. She sees the ring on his finger, and she holds out her hand, catching the rising sun's light on her wedding band. She holds them together, side by side.

But she wants to see his face. She wants to see his face.

He pushes his chin against her neck, and she feels his warm breath.

"I must remember this moment," she whispers to herself. "I must remember this moment forever."

And she does.

A strange, square light bends the space and time around her once again.

The moment fades, tearing her away from their ringed hands and the dawn. Other hands appear. Hands with trauma sheers cutting away her clothes, exposing her old naked body to the air. She does not care. She is still grasping the moment she swore she would always remember.

"*Please stop,*" she whispers. "*Please let me go back to him.*" But the words are trapped in her head.

A doctor stands over her. He has a beard. He talks in a loud, brusque voice, half shouting, half commanding.

"Mrs. Drader, can you squeeze my hand?" he yells. She feels a squeeze on her hand. She tries to squeeze it back, to make him go away, but her hand is somehow not hers.

"What about this hand?" the doctor shouts in her face. She feels a squeeze somewhere else. This time she does not try to squeeze back. She tries to die. She wills it with all her power and might. She prays, she cries to the sky, and she calls to him, "*Come get me. Let me be free of this place.*"

"*I want to see you. I want to see you.*"

Voices shout.

"She's doing it again!"

"Get me one hundred fifty milligrams of Amiodarone!" the doctor yells at the nurse.

He jams suction down into her mouth, and she realizes it is full of fluid and she can't breathe.

"We are going to intubate!" the doctor calls.

"Mrs. Drader, I am going to put a tube down your throat to keep you alive."

She gurgles out a response.

"Stay with us!" he yells at her. "Stay with us!"

"*Stay with us!*" she yells. "*Please, God, let him stay with us! Do not take him!*" She is sobbing. "*Stay with us!*" she yells again. But it is too late and she knows it. She is standing in a cold wind on the edge of a roaring stream. She holds the body of her only child, her son. She kneels and cries. She realizes it is the first moment in her life when she truly feels old.

But he is there again.

He rests a hand on her shoulder. She hears him sob, and she spins around, burying her face in his broad chest. His heart pounds against her ear, and she shakes as he shakes, and they shake together. He holds her with his strong arms, with arms that make her want to live.

"*I must remember this moment, too,*" she whispers to herself. "*I must remember this moment forever.*"

And she does.

He sobs with her, and the two of them stand alone. The same universe that felt so wonderful only minutes before now feels unbearably empty except for the two of them.

"*I will never leave you,*" she whispers to his chest. He kisses the top of her head. She lifts her face to kiss him back, but he is gone.

The doctor is screaming out doses and drugs. Some kind of nurse pins down over her mouth a bag that smells like old plastic. He squeezes a bag and it shoves air into her. She can feel them trying to force her to live. But with each memory, she feels the strands that tie her to this world loosening.

And it is wonderful.

The pain in her belly rears up again, and she feels it rip up all the way into her neck. This time it is a hot and burning sensation. She watches the pain with a detached curiosity. It irritates her that they are making such a mess because of her.

The pain comes again, and she recognizes suddenly that the pain is a friend. It can free her. She welcomes it. *"Please end this,"* she tells the pain.

The doctor pushes the bag off her mouth and shoves gloved fingers into her palate, ripping out her dentures. He jams the suction in once again, and its choking, sucking sound fills the air.

The world pulsates for a second and stops.

Two children sit on her lap. A boy and a girl. The twins. She hears herself talking to them. *"I will love you forever, no matter what,"* she says to one before turning to the other. *"I will love you forever, no matter what,"* she says again.

The children say it back together. *"And we will love you forever, no matter what."* They giggle and jump down off her lap, running over to the red and green presents stacked at the bottom of the Christmas tree.

A fire crackles and pops in a stone fireplace. A half-gone glass of milk sits on a plate with a note from Santa. "O Come, All Ye Faithful" plays out from the radio above the fire. It is Christmas morning. Lois watches the twins with such love that it feels as if her entire chest is glowing from joy. The children each pick up a present and sit down by the fire.

"Tell Daddy to hurry up!" The girl laughs.

"Wait for your father," she hears herself say. Everything in the room shines with life for her. We did this, she thinks. The two of

us made the two of them. We did this. Our love made this beautiful place.

This beautiful moment.

"I must remember this moment," she whispers to herself. "I must remember this moment forever."

And she does.

She hears him jogging down the hall. "Hang on, kids!" His voice! It is his voice! She wants to cry with delight at hearing his voice again. It has been so long since she's heard him speak. It is strong, clear, and healthy. She suddenly stands, tucking her hair back behind her ears, smoothing her pajamas, and grinning as she waits for him to come around the corner.

"Shocking!" the voice cries out.

She is pulled back to the present. The doctor stands over her with a big plastic tube in one hand and a metal blade in the other.

He nods, and the nurse injects something into her arm. It is a new sensation, and she tastes a bitter taste in her mouth. The pain in her chest and abdomen begin to drift away in a cloud of warmth.

She almost fades when she cries out in her mind, "*No! I don't want to be saved.*" She fights, but it is too much. The drugs submerge her into the warm dark.

Memories spin past now like snowflakes in a blizzard. They twirl, swirl, and roll about. Big memories and small memories. Soccer games, birthday parties, tears, laughter, camping trips, college acceptance letters, college rejection letters, an empty nest, and an empty home, and then, finally, it is just the two of them once again.

But he is there. She is not alone. He wraps thin arms around her. Thin arms. His giant frame feels like sticks as he clings to her chest in the hospital bed. His beautiful brown hair is gone, washed away from the never-ending rounds of chemo, radiation, and more chemo and more radiation.

She kisses his head ever so lightly. His skin still tastes of sea and pine. "*I must remember this moment,*" she whispers to herself. "*I must remember this moment forever.*"

And she does.

And then he is no more.

She floats back up to the surface of the dark. She can feel a tube in her throat and her lungs expanding and shrinking with the ventilator. She opens her eyes.

"She's waking up; give her more sedation," the doctor says. She is adrift within herself, the drugs clouding her mind.

The doctor is on the phone and he is yelling. He slams the receiver down. "Surgeon will be here in ten minutes. They are going to try to save her before it is too late." He sees her looking at him and he scowls.

"Jesus—she's awake." He looks disgusted. "Give her more Propofol, Dan." He turns back around and types at a computer. The nurse steps over to the IV pole and pushes some buttons. She feels the warmth coming back up her arm for her brain. She notices some red blood on the white pillow by her face.

It looks like a rose.

She is planting the rosebushes. Red roses for her, white roses for him. She is planting them side by side as she talks out loud to his memory. She digs down into the soil, planting the bush for him and the bush for her. Side by side. Every day the roses grow and she cares for them. The red roses and the white roses interlace together across the back of her yard.

It is their anniversary. She is picking roses to decorate the table. Tonight she will make his favorite meal and dine alone once again.

She picks up a rose and runs her fingers across the top of it. She feels the stem and how it rises to a sharp point. It pricks her finger, but she does not care; she is used to it. The stem buzzes, and she feels for it, suddenly remembering the bee. But this time it does not sting.

She is wheeling down a hall. People push her stretcher, running as fast as they can. They bash the stretcher into the operating room doors and run her into the operating room. Hands lift her body and drop her onto the cold black plastic mattress of the OR table.

"Let's go, let's go, let's go!" a surgeon yells as he scrubs his hands in a stainless-steel sink. "Her pressure's fifty—she's bleeding out!" He is frantic. They tear off the blankets, leaving her naked. A nurse dumps a bottle of Betadine across her distended abdomen. There is no time for proper procedure.

The surgeon gowns and gloves in a blur of motion. He grabs a scalpel.

He freezes. "Is she awake? Goddamn it, people."

Several other people swear out loud. Her IV became disconnected on the way to the OR. She is completely and totally awake on the ventilator, unable to move or cry out for help. Her eyes are open. They twinkle with joy. She is not looking at the surgeon or his blade or the bright lights.

She is looking at Henry.

He is here, just as she remembered him on the hill. He heard her call, and he has come for her. She sees his forest-green eyes, his beautiful, kind face, and his full head of hair. Their eyes meet. Joy ignites the room between them in a blinding white light. He is young and strong and old and wise at the same moment. She smells the pine and the sea. She knows now it really is him.

He smiles at her and extends his hand.

She sits up, out of her body, forgetting about the ventilator, about the ninety-one years, about the medications pumping through her, about the body she is suddenly leaving behind.

The pain in her abdomen is gone.

The surgeon is screaming, alarms are ringing, nurses are yelling, but all she hears is the sound of waves breaking on the surf in the distance. The moon is rising, casting its off-white path across the surface of the sea toward the horizon.

She knows now where it leads.

She reaches out her hand and sees that it is just how she remembered it. It is healthy and young and strong, but also old and wise at the same time, just like his.

They touch.

He leans forward and kisses her gently. She tastes the sea, the sky, and the trees swaying in a summer wind.

He takes her hand in his, and she walks by his side toward the distant moon shining across the surface of the sea.

A child appears.

He is running to her.

"*Mommy!*" he cries. "*Mommy!*"

She lifts him with ease into her arms, setting him on her hip, where he always used to be before the creek took him. Her sisters arrive. Her mother, her father—one by one they welcome her to the new place.

She has already forgotten the feeling of pain in this life.

Now it is only the touch of Henry's hand that she feels.

"*I must remember this moment,*" she whispers to herself. "*I must remember this moment forever.*"

And she will.

The surgeon is tearing off his gloves, the nurses are turning off monitors, and a blanket is gently pulled up over an empty, wrinkled body.

Her life has ended.

It is a beautiful thing.

Made in the USA
Columbia, SC
02 May 2017